No mercy. . . .

Fargo felt one bullet graze his temple, the other his shoulder, and knew he was falling from the saddle. He struck the ground hard, snapping away the film that had begun to fall over his eyes. He shook his head to clear it and had just enough time to glimpse a huge man charging him in a fury. He kicked Fargo, sending him flying. He winced at the pain in his shoulder, and his vision grew foggy again. Sensing the man advancing, Fargo rolled, striking his head against a tree, the shock clearing his vision. He looked up to see Sam Eakins standing over him, a thick length of branch in one hand. Eakins swung the branch, smashing into Fargo's side.

Eakins panted, "I ain't gonna kill you, mister. That'd be too good for you. But what I will do is bust you up so you can't walk, run, or even raise your hands again. I'm gonna smash your spine in two!"

He raised the branch and swung with all his might at the Trailsman's back. . . .

THE
TRAILSMAN
#223

IDAHO
GHOST TOWN

by

Jon Sharpe

A SIGNET BOOK

SIGNET
Published by New American Library, a division of
Penguin Putnam Inc., 375 Hudson Street,
New York, New York 10014, U.S.A.
Penguin Books Ltd, 27 Wrights Lane,
London W8 5TZ, England
Penguin Books Australia Ltd,
Ringwood, Victoria, Australia
Penguin Books Canada Ltd, 10 Alcorn Avenue,
Toronto, Ontario, Canada M4V 3B2
Penguin Books (N.Z.) Ltd, 182–190 Wairau Road,
Auckland 10, New Zealand

Penguin Books Ltd, Registered Offices:
Harmondsworth, Middlesex, England

First published by Signet, an imprint of New American Library,
a division of Penguin Putnam Inc.

First Printing, May 2000
10 9 8 7 6 5 4 3 2 1

The first chapter of this book originally appeared in *Colorado Diamond Dupe*,
the two hundred twenty-second volume in this series.

Ⓢ REGISTERED TRADEMARK—MARCA REGISTRADA

Printed in the United States of America

PUBLISHER'S NOTE
This is a work of fiction. Names, characters, places, and incidents are
either the product of the author's imagination or are used fictitiously,
and any resemblance to actual persons, living or dead, business
establishments, events, or locales is entirely coincidental.

The Trailsman

Beginnings . . . they bend the tree and they mark the man. Skye Fargo was born when he was eighteen. Terror was his midwife, vengeance his first cry. Killing spawned Skye Fargo, ruthless, cold-blooded murder. Out of the acrid smoke of gunpowder still hanging in the air, he rose, cried out a promise never forgotten.

The Trailsman they began to call him all across the West: searcher, scout, hunter, the man who could see where others only looked, his skills for hire but not his soul, the man who lived each day to the fullest, yet trailed each tomorrow. Skye Fargo, the Trailsman, the seeker who could take the wildness of a land and the wanting of a woman and make them his own.

*Southern Idaho, 1860—at the
lower edge of the Salmon River Mountains,
where the eerie remnants of a ghost town
not-so-long forgotten took on a new
and deadly facade. . . .*

The big man's lake blue eyes swept the rich, lush terrain that throbbed with cottonwoods, silver aspen, junipers, hackberry, blue spruce, and a dozen variety of pine. This was land that welcomed the golden eagle and the mountain lion, the bighorn sheep, and the sagebrush vole, a land that played host to the largest and the smallest of creatures. It was a place of beauty that should have fostered relaxation and calm. Yet the trailsman was neither relaxed nor calm. He had ridden in enough such places to know that beauty could be a mask for death. The brilliant red, yellow, and black coral snake came to mind, as did the soft seductive loveliness of the pitcher plant. There were plenty of others that cloaked death in their appealing visage.

But it was more than that causing his uneasiness, Skye Fargo realized. When you became a trailsman, he had long ago learned, you came to know more than the ways of the wild, the specific wisdom of signs and marks, of bush, flower, wind, sun, and earth. You come to develop a special sensitivity, a kind of sixth sense that lets you respond to the unseen, the unheard, and the unsaid. It was a kind of sensitivity that enabled you to stay alive, he had learned. To be a trailsman was to be part of, yet apart from everything around you. It was a feat only the red man had mastered, he had come to realize. And now, as he slowly rode the rich land, he felt that sixth sense bring the uneasiness that rode with him. Nothing he could see, hear, smell, or touch. Yet it was there in the hairs standing on the back of his neck.

After all, for all its rich, full beauty, this was Shoshoni country. Some northern Paiute and Bannock strayed across this land, but it was the Shoshoni who ruled here, embracing and drawing strength and protection from the great Sawtooth Range to the west, and the Salmon River Mountains to the north and east. The Oregon and California trails had been blazed through these mountains to the north. But enough pioneers left the trails to find places for themselves in the richness of the land. Towns took root, nourished by those who abandoned the long trails westward. Some grew and flourished, others barely clung to existence. But to all, the Shoshoni were a constant threat. To the Shoshoni, these people were a constant intrusion, as unwelcome as wasps at a feast.

So in this land of rich beauty, relaxation was a dicey thing at best, enjoyment a gift never taken for granted. Uneasiness clinging to him, Fargo moved the Ovaro along a narrow deer trail, one side lined with blue spruce, the other side overlooking a small plateau. The Ovaro's jet black fore-and-hindquarters glistened in the sun, its cream white midsection gleaming as the horse rounded a slow curve in the trail. But the horse's ears were twitching, Fargo noted, echoing the hairs that were stiff on the back of his own neck. The sudden sharp cry that cut through the air was the high-pitched sound of a child's voice. Fargo pushed the pinto into a trot and peered down at the small plateau only a dozen feet below.

Five men on horseback and one on foot surrounded a young Indian girl who wore only a brief length of hide around her waist. Perhaps ten years old, Fargo guessed, little budding breasts just beginning to appear on her small, slender frame. The man on foot, a torn Stetson on his head, held the little girl by her arms. A reed basket filled with camass lay on the ground beside her as she struggled helplessly to tear away from the man. "Look what we got here," the man in the torn Stetson said. "We got us a little flower ready to be plucked."

"You don't mean *plucked,* Harry," one of the others said and they all joined in harsh laughter. They began to swing from their horses. One of them, a tall, thin man, just touched the ground with his right foot when the arrow hurtled into him, never letting him get his left foot down. The arrow disappeared through his back almost to the feathers on the shaft. The man slumped to the ground with a last gasp of breath rushing from his lips, a sound not unlike a balloon deflating. The others spun as a second arrow cleaved the air, grazing the man holding the little girl as he managed to twist away.

A scream of rage followed the arrows and Fargo saw an Indian pony charge into view. A young woman leaned forward as she rode, her elkskin dress hiked up over her knees to reveal shapely legs. It was custom for the one-piece dresses of Indian women to be cut differently along the bottom hemline according to tribe. Fargo instantly spotted the long, curved line that marked the Shoshoni dresses. Her handsome face strained in fury. She raced the pony forward as she fired another arrow at the men. She missed entirely with this one, though, and Fargo saw the men had their guns drawn to fire. But immediately, she was leaping headlong from the back of her pony, flinging herself at the man in the torn Stetson, who had seized hold of the little girl again. Fargo glimpsed the flash of the hunting knife in the woman's hand. The man dove away from her as her blade sliced the air hardly more than an inch from his chest. Before she could draw her arm back to flash again, his kick caught her in the stomach.

The young woman went down, gasping for breath, and the man with the torn Stetson was atop her at once, wrestling the knife from her, throwing her onto her back and steadying himself atop her. "Look at this now. We've got two pigeons to enjoy," he said as one of the others seized the little girl.

"Let's take the little one, first. Sort of like an appetizer," one of the others said to a chorus of laughs. Fargo drew his Colt as he moved the Ovaro forward. He knew the face of brutality and savagery. He'd seen the Indian practice his own brand of it. Brutality was a universal sickness and Fargo had no tolerance for it, no matter who played at it. Besides, in this Shoshoni country, a brutal attack on two Indian girls could explode into a lot of innocent people being killed. Yet he knew nothing about these men. Maybe they were simply the usual garden variety scum. He'd give them a chance to keep their lives, he decided, and sent the Ovaro forward down the small slope to the plateau.

The men were concentrating on their two captives and Fargo saw the young woman's eyes flash with black hatred at the man in the torn Stetson. Fargo fired as the Ovaro reached the plateau, purposely aiming his shot to smash into the ground at the foot of the man wearing the Stetson. A small spray of dirt flew into the air and the men spun in surprise, seeing him instantly as he sent the Ovaro closer. "Let her go. The little girl, too," Fargo said almost softly.

"Son of a bitch, who the hell are you?" the torn Stetson growled.

"Nobody. Just let them go," Fargo said.

"You some goddamn Indian lover?" the man rasped.

"Let them go. Find yourselves some saloon girls," Fargo said.

"We've found what we want," the man said. "You've got ten seconds to ride or you're a dead man."

Fargo swore under his breath. They were too bent on pleasure to listen and too dumb to notice that he had positioned himself at the edge of the spruce. He counted off the seconds as his eyes moved back and forth at their hands. He was ready as he saw one go for his gun, the others just starting to yank at theirs. He had the Colt in hand in a blink, letting it bark twice as two of the figures toppled from their horses as if they'd been hauled off together by an invisible rope. He was already diving from the Ovaro as the others began to send a hail of bullets his way. He hit the ground inside the spruce, rolled, and came up on his stomach to return fire. But before he got off another shot, a half-dozen Indian ponies appeared at the other edge of the plateau.

They came firing both arrows and rifles and the four remaining men vaulted onto their horses and raced away, leaving the young woman and the little girl behind. Fargo rose, stepped out of the spruce, and saw the near-naked Shoshoni were already running down the four fleeing riders. He walked toward the young woman, the little girl now clinging to her, as another six braves charged into sight. They raced right at him, and had him surrounded in seconds. Fargo stayed motionless, letting his arms hang loosely, the Colt still in his right hand. He took in the pointed arrows poised on drawn bowstrings and kept his face expressionless.

Fargo's eyes went to the young woman as she came forward, speaking to the six braves in a firm voice. One of the bucks answered her in anger, yet a hint of uncertainty caught in his voice. But the Indian girl's tone became sharper, more commanding, and he saw the braves lower their bows. Fargo allowed himself to draw a deep sigh of relief as the young woman continued to talk with them. He wished they spoke Siouan, which the Crow, Assiniboin, Osage and many other tribes used as a working language. He knew Siouan well enough, as he did Kiowa and Pawnee. But the Shoshoni spoke Shoshonean, one of the tongues in which Fargo only knew a few words, so he remained silent and tried to catch a word here and there. It also gave him a chance to really see the young woman for the first time and he found himself looking at a smooth-skinned face of uncommon handsomeness, almost a classic kind of beauty.

High cheekbones gave her face strong planes, her nose aquiline, her lips a delicate line. Her black, liquid eyes gazed back at him, contrasting strikingly with her coppery tinged skin. Her elk-skin shirt was pushed forward enough to indicate full, high breasts and he'd already glimpsed shapely legs. The first six braves returned to interrupt his admiration of her handsomeness and she turned to them, again speaking in commanding tones. The braves fell into line with the others and finally, she turned to Fargo. "Come with me," she said and started to walk, the little girl still clinging at her side.

"You speak English," he said in surprise.

"Some. Our medicine man taught me. He learned from Crow bluecoat scouts," she said. He nodded and knew that Indian Cavalry scouts often taught the white man's tongue to their own people, who in turn taught it to others.

"How are you called?" Fargo asked as he walked beside the young woman and led the Ovaro behind him.

"Awenita," she said. "Fawn, in your tongue."

"Fawn . . . Awenita," Fargo repeated. "Nice. And the little one?

"Cholena . . . bird," she answered. "You?"

"Fargo," he said.

She gave him a slow, appraising glance. "Fargo," she said, rolling the name on her tongue. "Strong man. Strong name." She swung onto her pony with smooth grace, motioning for him to climb onto the Ovaro. Holding the child on the pony in front of her, she led the way through blue spruce, a stand of silver aspen and finally, a long, thick forest of white fir. The child held on to the basket with the camass in it. They had obviously been out picking squash when the men had found them, unaware there were braves nearby. Maybe the braves would have come on to the scene before it was too late, Fargo realized. Then again, maybe not. He was glad he'd intervened, though the warriors riding behind in stony silence were more than a little unnerving.

Perhaps another half hour went by when the trees thinned out and he saw the large camp appear, consisting of at least a dozen teepees, many fire pits, drying racks, and, he guessed, another sixty braves, squaws, and children. This was no hunting camp, Fargo thought. This was a full base camp with a wide stream running alongside it, providing constant fresh water. Awenita rode into the camp with him as others quickly came forward in curiosity. She halted before a tall teepee with many drawings of battle exploits painted on it. As the other braves gathered around, Fargo was struck by how all had the same high-planed faces, the same strong, well-built bodies, the same proud presence.

He was reminded of the fact that the Shoshoni were one of the four tribes with the highest percentage of full-bloods. Marrying out of the tribe was against their code. The flap of the teepee opened, interrupting his thoughts, and a tall, imposing figure stepped out, bare-chested, clad only in deerskin leggings. Two golden eagle feathers were in his long, shiny black hair. The man glared at Fargo with both curiosity and dislike and Awenita glanced at Fargo. "My father, chief of the Shoshoni. He is called Wamblee," she said.

"Eagle," Fargo said and her eyes widened in surprise.

"You know Shoshoni?" she asked.

"A few words," Fargo said. One of the braves who had ridden back with them spoke up quickly, his words terse, and Fargo saw the chief listen with his face expressionless. When the brave finished, Awenita spoke, impatience and dismissal in her tone. Again, the chief listened and nodded when she finished and turned to Fargo.

"I told my father that the braves did not see what

you did. They are wrong in what they thought," she said.

"Hope he believes you," Fargo said.

"He knows I do not speak falsely. I am his daughter," she said imperiously. The Shoshoni chief interrupted, his gaze piercing as he addressed Fargo. Awenita translated when he finished. "He asks why. They were your people. Why did you stop them?" she queried. "I ask it, too."

Fargo understood the question behind the question and he groped for words that would answer them both. "They wanted to do bad. I stop bad things, no matter who does them," he said. The Indian girl took a moment to translate the answer and when she did, the chief grunted but did not soften his piercing gaze. When he spoke, Awenita again translated.

"My father says there will be no forgetting or forgiving the attack on Cholena and me. It is one more thing your people will pay for. But you have shown you are not like the others. For this, you will live. For this good thing you have done, I will do what our ways tell me to do, he has said." When she finished, the chief turned and strode into his tent and the crowd of braves and squaws began to disperse. Fargo felt the deep breath of relief slide from his lips. This much was over and he still had his scalp. "Come," Awenita said and he followed her as she moved through the camp. She was well named, he decided, her movements delicate and fawnlike with soft, poised steps. She led him to another of the tall tents and held the flap open for him to enter. Inside, he saw a half-dozen blankets covering the floor. A small fire inside a pit of stones threw a soft light inside the tent. "My teepee. It will be dark soon. You can spend the night here."

"Thanks," he said.

"It is I who give thanks for what you did for me, and for Cholena," the Indian girl said. "Rest. I will return. My teepee is yours."

She slipped quickly and silently from the tent and the night descended soon after. He stretched out on the blankets and found them soft and comfortable. He sat up only when the tent flap opened and Awenita entered. She carried two stone bowls of food, along with two stone spoons, and knelt down beside him to give him one of the bowls. He saw mashed camass, berries, and corn kernels all mixed together in a thick liquid that tasted of ground nuts and honey. "Good," he said as he ate. Awenita smiled and there was a softness in her face he had not seen before. She leaned back when the meal ended, resting on both elbows, and the elkskin dress crept up enough to show Fargo her lovely, slow-curving thighs.

"I am here for you," she said. "It is our way. A great kindness, a special deed, must be repaid."

"No need for that," Fargo answered.

"You gave me my life. It was a special gift. I give you myself. It is the greatest offering I have to give," she said simply.

"I'm honored," Fargo said, and was about to say more when she stood up, pulled the elkskin garment off over her head to stand naked before him. He felt the sudden intake of his breath at her loveliness, his eyes roaming over a perfectly balanced figure, every part of her completely in proportion with every other part. Long, lovely legs moved into narrow hips; a lean, flat belly joined a narrow waist, and his eyes lingered on modest breasts, each tipped by a small, coppery pink point. Even her little pubic V was neat and small and entirely symmetrical, keeping with the rest of her.

"Do I please you?" she asked simply.

"Does the flower please the bee?" he answered. "But that doesn't matter." She frowned and Fargo felt a strange thing happening to himself. He'd always made it a rule never to turn down a free drink or a willing woman. It was one of the keystones of his personal philosophy of life. Yet he suddenly felt the need to turn away from this willing and beautiful girl. He sure as hell didn't want to, he realized, but his intuition was working against him, that old sixth sense pulling hard at him. She felt she owed him a personal debt. More than that, a Shoshoni chief owed him a major debt. In this country, that was better than money in the bank.

Something told him it was a debt he shouldn't use up, not here, not now. He was riding into a territory where he should hang on to a little extra insurance if he could. He brought his eyes to her waiting, deep brown orbs. "Another time," he said.

A furrow dug into her brow at once. "Why?" she asked. "It is my gift to you for what you did. It is our way."

"I know and I understand," he said, hunting for words she would understand yet wouldn't anger or hurt her. The thought of returning to collect the debt was more than a little appealing, he reminded himself and finally he found words as Awenita's eyes stayed fastened on him. "This is something you do now because it is a thing of honor, and the way of your people. But I want you to do it only because you want to, not out of honor, not because it's the way of your people, but your way, from inside your heart. Do you know what I say?"

She stayed silent for a long moment, peering hard at him. "I must think more," she said slowly. "We sleep, now." She pulled the dress back on and lay down on a blanket on the other side of the teepee. He swore silently, stretched out on the blanket, and slept only after he heard the even sounds of her soft snores.

When dawn came, he woke, rose, and glanced at her. The elkskin dress had crept up to reveal most of one lovely leg, the planes of her face now more tranquil than strong and giving her a more ethereal beauty. It took an added push of willpower for him to slip from the teepee, and he was halfway to the Ovaro when he heard her step from the teepee, the tent flap making a soft slap as she pulled it back. He halted as she came to him.

"I have thought. I know what your words told me," she said. "I understand and it is good. When will you come back?"

He gave her a puzzled look.

"It will not just be for the honor and our ways, then," she said.

"I'll be back, then," he said and climbed into the saddle as the camp began to wake. He felt her eyes on him as he slowly rode from the camp and only when he vanished into the deep of the forest did he feel her eyes stop following him. The Shoshoni chief would honor the uncollected debt, Fargo knew, and now his daughter had added something more to the pot. He put the pinto into a trot. Suddenly he wanted to finish whatever had brought him here as quickly as he could. The thought abruptly brought him back to the fact that he didn't know what he had come here to find. He had a letter in his pocket and with it had come a very generous payment and some directions, but nothing more. It wasn't the kind of money to turn down and his curiosity had been aroused. So he had come here into the Salmon Mountains' wildness, a land that defied breaking new trails through its lush and rugged terrain.

He found a pond, washed up, and ate from a bush of wild plums before going on. He went over the letter's instructions in his mind.

Go to a town called Eakins. From there, follow the Yellow River north to Grange. I will meet you in Grange. You'll know Grange because it's right between two big stands of Bigcone spruce where the Yellow River makes a sharp turn east.

B. Baker

He'd ridden some of this territory before, and though he'd never visited Eakins, he had heard of the town. Fargo headed northwest until the day ran out. Finding a cluster of hackberry, he bedded down after unsaddling the Ovaro and tethering the horse beside a tiny but fast-running stream. Hunger gnawed at him, so he rose and made a small fire with some nearby twigs, then heated a strip of cold beef jerky out of his saddlebag. When he finished, he felt better and stretched out again, finally falling asleep.

The sudden, loud panicked neighing of the Ovaro woke him, and he sprang up at once. His eyes flashed to the horse, where the half-moon's light showed the animal tugging at its tether. It was then he saw the furry shapes nearby and heard their low growls. Timber wolves, he saw at once, counting at least ten. They were creeping around the edges of the little area where he had made camp. Fargo was beside the Ovaro in a half-dozen long strides. As he used his touch to calm the horse, he drew the big Henry from its saddle case, then turned and moved a few feet toward the wolves, the rifle up and ready to fire. The moonlight let him pick out the leader of the pack, a large dark gray wolf who moved closer as the others followed. They had picked up his scent, of course, and that of the remains of his food.

The pack began to encircle him in their usual, cautious manner, and then the leader suddenly darted forward. Fargo fired off a shot and the wolf, swerving, avoided the bullet. He swerved again, avoiding Fargo's second shot. He was drawing back as two others at the ends of the half circle came forward in a darting crouch. They were hard to see against the trees in the poor light, and Fargo fired off two more shots for effect more than anything else. The two wolves drew back and the pack leader, followed by another three, made a quick run toward him from the side, the three with him spreading out as they followed. Fargo swung the rifle and fired another two shots, hearing one of the wolves yelp. The leader drew back at once and, following his moves, they began to circle him with their loping gait.

They edged closer and a few made another try at coming directly at him, but fell back as soon as he fired. They kept circling, their attempts to attack seemingly halfhearted. Fargo felt the furrow dig into his brow. He was a perfect target for them, alone and outnumbered. Even with the rifle, he'd not be able to stand off a quick, concentrated attack from all sides.

He fully expected that's what they'd do and he was prepared to swing the rifle and lay down a circle of fire. But they continued to make only fitful half charges, drawing back the moment he brought the rifle up to fire. Deciding not to play victim any longer, he sent off a volley of shots, spraying them in a half circle. The wolves crouched, backed, ran, and re-formed.

But they didn't circle him again and they didn't mount a real charging attack. Instead, after a few more moments of desultory growling, they began to lope away. Fargo watched them go, the frown remaining on his brow. As they disappeared into the trees he realized there was only one reason they'd passed up such a perfect victim: They weren't really hungry. Something else had satisfied their needs. He grunted with a bitter gratefulness. But when he returned to his bedroll, he reloaded the Henry and kept it at his side as he slept. The Ovaro would awaken him again if they crept their way back, but he didn't anticipate they would. It was not their way. He slept again until the morning birdsongs woke him. He rose, washed, and drank from his canteen and walked to where the pawprints of the wolves were plain at the edges of his little campsite.

The line of prints revealed they had come to the camp from the northeast. He took the Ovaro and followed. The wolf tracks kept moving northeast, then suddenly turned northwest. Fargo reined up, dismounted, and stared at two graves that had been dug up by the pack. He also saw the remains of two corpses, one a man, the other a woman, both more than half eaten by the pack. They had been lying in shallow graves, Fargo saw. The pack had easily picked up the scent of the two bodies and quickly dug them up. Hungry wolves were not averse to a little carrion. His eyes narrowed as he scanned the graves again. These were not the graves of settlers who had died and were buried by their friends. Nor were they from a passing wagon train. Those graves would have been deeper. They would also have been marked. These were unmarked by even the most primitive of wooden crosses.

Fargo returned to the Ovaro and rode on, but a distinct feeling of unease stayed with him. Unmarked graves were usually consigned to the worst of the worst, unsavory bodies dumped in a potter's field section of a town graveyard. What had brought this man and this woman to such an ignoble burial? Fargo wondered. He only knew one thing—they had not been buried for long. The scent the wolves had picked up proved that point. Putting the pinto into a trot, he rode on, ignoring the trail of the pack as it turned west. He rode through country that was both rolling and mountainous, yet with enough open land to attract anyone wanting to start a modest farm. He rode for quite a while before he saw a man in a lone buckboard and steered the horse over to the traveler.

"Afternoon," Fargo began pleasantly. "You know these parts?"

"Ought to. Live nearby," said the man, an elderly figure with a tired face.

"Looking for a town named Eakins," Fargo said.

"Keep heading northwest. You'll come to it," the man said.

"Been a funeral around here lately?" Fargo asked.

"Lots of funerals around here all the time," the man said. "Depends on who gets Sam Eakins riled up."

Fargo allowed a wry smile. It was an answer both

informative and cautionary. "Much obliged," he said and sent the pinto forward. He rode on, wondering if the couple in the unmarked graves had gotten Sam Eakins riled up. He wouldn't pursue the thought. Eakins was not his destination, only a marking spot on the way to Grange. But his uneasiness continued to persist and he swore silently as he hurried on.

2

Following the man's directions, Fargo stayed north and west and it was well into the afternoon when the land opened up, and he began to pass barns and houses. He saw a pig farm, two small vegetable plots, and a half-dozen more homes with two still being built. People had set down roots here and Fargo knew he oughtn't to be surprised. Pioneers wrapped themselves in their own ambitions, all too often without regard for reality. The Salmon River Mountain country was forbidding wildness despite its rich beauty. Prime, pristine land offered rich soils fit for growing almost anything. Deer, elk, mountain goat, raccoon, wild turkey, pheasant, and a host of other creatures offered a natural larder.

As his road widened, Fargo saw heavy tread marks. More than a few families had come this way on their heavy Conestogas, all seeking a new beginning. Soon he found the road passing close to low hills where neatly hoed rows of squash, zucchini, eggplant, and lettuce grew in straight lines. A man with a full, red beard paused in his hoeing to wave and Fargo rode up to him, reining to a halt. Two little boys and a pleasant-faced woman came out from a house and approached.

"Just passing through?" the man said, his square, open face peering at him over his fiery beard.

"More or less," Fargo said.

"Jed Hopper," the man said. "My wife, Amy, and this here's Luke and Paul."

"Skye Fargo. A lot more of you in these parts?" Fargo questioned.

"More this side of Eakins, some on the other side. We've sort of got our own little community here in these low hills, as you can see," Jed Hopper said.

"The Shoshoni give you trouble?" Fargo asked.

"Not yet, though I heard they wiped out a community south of here in the valley. But we plan to handle them if they come," Jed Hopper said.

Fargo's brows lifted but he kept his voice casual. "How?" he asked.

"Look at the houses up behind me," the man said, gesturing with one arm. "You see they're all built in a half circle?"

"I do," Fargo said. "I can't see how that'll help you fight off the Shoshoni, though."

"You know anything about Indian fighting, Fargo?" Jed Hopper queried.

"More than I want to remember, from one end of this land to the other. There's hardly a tribe I haven't fought," Fargo said.

"That's real impressive. But our houses are our own idea. We can all see each other. We can all see what's happened at each other's land. Which means we can all cover each other's houses. Any damn Shoshoni attacks one of these houses, they'll find bullets coming at him from every other house. We can lay down a right good barrage."

"I imagine you can," Fargo said as thoughts ran

through his mind. He thought of telling Jed Hopper how their plans would be useless, how they had fashioned amateur plans out of their own inexperience. But he put these thoughts aside. They didn't know him well enough to listen to him and he hadn't the time to tell them what they ought to be doing. "Hope it all works the way you've set it up. Good luck to you," he said instead and moved the pinto on.

But his pleasant smile vanished as he rode on. These were good people who had no idea what they faced. They had never seen an all-out Indian attack; not by the Shoshoni, not by the Cheyenne, the Crow, or any of the other fierce warrior tribes. They had no idea of the fury that awaited them. They had no idea that the Shoshoni wouldn't attack one house and let them lay down a protective barrage from the other houses. They had no realization that the Shoshoni had probably already seen through their pitiful attempt at self-protection. Maybe one day, when he finished with whatever had brought him here, he'd return and straighten out their misconceptions.

He rode on, not knowing whether to admire their courage or scream at their foolhardiness. But this was a country being carved out by dreamers and fools, and it was hard to tell one from the other.

The terrain stayed open as he rode on along the wide trail until finally he saw the buildings of the town rise up in front of him. Eakins turned out to be a larger town than he'd expected and he rode slowly down the wide main street, passing a number of Owensboro mountain wagons, buckboards, and a few one-horse surreys. He also saw the Eakins General Store, Eakins Wheelwright, Eakins Bank, Eakins Blacksmith, and the town saloon and dance hall, which was named the Eakins Pleasure Palace. It was very plain who owned this town and Fargo felt the distaste stirring inside him. He never liked to see too much power in one man's hands. It usually brought out the worst in human nature. The words of the man in the buckboard came into his thoughts. Apparently, Sam Eakins was not only a man of power. He was not a man to rile.

When he reached the end of the town, Fargo saw three long bunkhouse buildings along with a corral and a barn. Some thirty men were both inside and outside the corral and he saw ten more just arriving. Some of the men were doing personal chores, some pitching horseshoes, others lounging about. He rode up to a half-dozen figures leaning against the corral fence, instantly seeing that they were scruffy, hard-eyed men, drifters for hire, the kind whose every manner showed no hint of having ever been loyal to anything. In a far corner of the corral he spotted a large, heavy dray with chain-linked stake sides, filled with shovels, axes, picks, sluices, and every sort of prospecting equipment.

Halting, he nodded at the six men, who returned uninviting, cold stares. "Looking for the Yellow River. Want to find a town named Grange," Fargo said.

Instant surprise swam into their faces, Fargo saw. "Grange?" one echoed.

"He never heard of it," the one beside him said, a pasty-faced character.

"He can't talk for himself?" Fargo asked the second one.

The pasty-faced one poked the other one in the ribs. "Go on, Eddie, tell him yourself."

"Never heard of it," the first one said obediently.

Fargo's eyes narrowed as they swept the others. "Any of you heard of it? It's somewhere in these parts," he said.

"No such place," a third figure answered.

"Yep, no such place," another echoed.

Fargo's eyes stayed on the men. Their sudden nervous unease was almost palpable. Why? he wondered, but he knew they'd not be giving him any reasons. He moved the Ovaro on behind a line of aspen and halted to peer out through the trees. He saw three of the men had left the corral and were running back to a big, imposing house some twenty yards beyond. Fargo moved on as they rushed inside the house, keeping east until he suddenly came upon the river. It flowed north along the other side of the town, screened by a thick growth of Gambel oak. He immediately saw why the Yellow River had been named as such. A small creek, its bubbling waters had a distinctly yellow tinge. Swinging alongside the river, he followed its path as it curved and straightened, winding its way through high hills, dense on both sides with hackberry, junipers, and cottonwoods.

The incident with the men clung to Fargo as he rode, their response to his question certainly strange. But he was becoming used to strange and unexpected things on this trip, and the Shoshoni girl once again leaped into his mind. Perhaps the strange note that had brought him here had set the tone, he mused as his eyes swept the hills on both sides of the amber waterway. He'd gone perhaps another half mile when his eyes picked up movement in the hills to his right, a slight rustle the ordinary rider would never have detected. But his eyes were the Trailsman's eyes, trained to see as the hawk sees, with that special awareness of all wild things.

The leaves of the cottonwoods had moved. But not by a puff of wind, his eyes had told him at once. Even a mild breeze would cause the leaves to move in a line, pushed by a ripple of wind. These leaves had moved in separate little places and as he glanced out of the corner of his eye he saw them move again. Someone was behind them, peering out, moving the dense screen of the foliage in order to see better. Fargo decided he'd had enough of the unexpected, enough surprises, and he turned the Ovaro sharply, cut across the shallow water of the Yellow River, and spurred the horse up into the hills. The cottonwoods closed in around him at once and he slowed, peering forward. Whoever watched had seen him cross the river and go up into the hills, of course, but Fargo stayed still and swept the denseness of the forest ahead. He caught the movement of the leaves again, a brushing movement this time, lower on the trees than he'd expected. Whoever had watched him had decided to slip away. Fargo slid from the Ovaro, landed silently on the ground, and crept forward on foot.

He swept the forest with narrowed eyes, listening yet hearing nothing. A furrow pressed into his brow, and he drew deeply of the forest air. He took a few steps forward, halted, and drew in a deep breath again. He had assumed a horseman had been behind the leaves he'd seen move from below. But no smell of horse drifted to his nostrils, no scent of fur or leather. The furrow became a frown as he listened for the sound of a rein chain, perhaps the soft plod of a hoof. Again, he heard nothing. He was still frowning and listening when the shot exploded through the trees. Fargo felt the bullet graze his temple as he fell forward, landing facedown on the ground. His arms outstretched, he lay as if dead as the line of blood trickled down his temple.

But as he lay motionless, holding his breath, he peered through the tiny slits of his half-closed eyes. The soft sound of the footsteps came toward him and he saw a foot come into sight near his hand. An ankle and lower leg swam into his view, then the tip of a rifle barrel. But the barrel was pointed down at the ground, away from him. Gathering his muscles, Fargo's arm lashed out with the speed of a rattler's strike. His arm closed around the ankle and he pulled with all the strength of his powerful deltoids, twisting his body as he did for added leverage. As the figure came crashing down beside him, Fargo closed both hands around the rifle and yanked it away. He stared in disbelief at the figure's wavy, dark brown hair, at the dirt-smudged cheeks that couldn't hide a pretty, snub-nosed face.

"I'll be damned," he breathed as the young woman pushed back, sat up, and glared at him out of brown eyes that held more fury than fright in them. "Who the hell are you?" Fargo said as they pushed to their feet. She was of medium height, in torn jeans and a wrinkled shirt that rested on modest, high breasts.

"You know damn well," she hissed.

"No, I don't," Fargo said. "And I don't know why you damn near killed me."

"I'm sorry I missed." She glowered. "You were looking for me and you found me. You got lucky. You don't need to play games about it."

"I'm not playing games and I wasn't looking for

you. I rode up here to see who was watching me from the hills," he said. She was frowning at him in confusion when he heard the sound of horses from below. Fargo peered through the trees and saw six riders halted at the bank of the river. He recognized them immediately as the men he'd talked to outside Eakins, the pasty-faced one in the lead. The man gestured at the Ovaro's hoofprints along the riverbank.

"He crossed here," the man said. "We'll get him. He can't be too far ahead."

Fargo watched the riders start to cross the river and brought his eyes to the girl. "Get under that grape bush over there," he said. "Lay flat and be quiet. There are going to be a lot of bullets flying around here soon enough." She hesitated, her eyes holding on him. "Now, dammit!" he barked and she turned and started to run the dozen feet to the bush, her round little rear bouncing under the torn jeans. He watched until she slid out of sight, then he returned his eyes to the Ovaro. He strode to the horse, took the big Henry from its saddle case, and positioned himself behind the trunk of a wide old cottonwood. A few moments later, the six riders reached the trees and pushed their way into the forest.

"He's not far away," the pasty-faced one said to the others. "If you see him, shoot."

Fargo's lips pulled back in a grimace. Why were they here chasing after him? All he had done was ask simple directions. It made no damn sense, Fargo murmured. But they were very serious, Fargo saw as he noted a six-gun in each man's hand. As they moved carefully through the trees, Fargo raised the rifle. They were in his sights, these strangers out to hunt him down. They were easy targets for the fast-firing Henry.

But he'd never had much stomach for killing in cold blood. He knew he was risking his life but old habits cling to a man.

"Drop your guns and nobody gets hurt," Fargo called out.

The pasty-faced one's eyes widened in surprise but he brought his revolver up, and started to spray bullets in the general direction of Fargo's voice. But Fargo had the rifle aimed and the big Henry barked. The pasty-faced man jiggled in the saddle before he toppled from his horse. The Henry was barking again before he hit the ground. Three more shots and two of the others fell from their mounts. The other three were firing but there was fear and hesitancy in their shots. Fargo dropped flat and fired from his stomach as one of the three started to wheel his horse to flee. The man went only a few feet before he flew from his horse as the rifle exploded again. One of the last two leaped to the ground and tried to race for the conceal-ment of the high brush. His race ended as he lay shud-dering, draped across the brush until he slowly slid to the ground.

The last man stayed in the saddle, and turned his horse into the trees as Fargo pushed to his feet. Glimpsing the fleeing rider moving through the trees, Fargo saw that the man was racing back the way he'd come. He thought about trying to give chase on the Ovaro and quickly discarded the thought. The man had too much of a head start. Instead, Fargo stepped to the edge of the trees where he had first peered down at the river to see the men as they arrived. He only had a moment to wait when the fleeing rider came into sight, nosing his horse down the incline toward the river. Fargo raised the rifle, pushed aside the leaves and branches, and paused to line up his sights. Cursing his own weakness, he shouted down, to the man.

"Rein up, dammit!" he ordered. The man half turned in the saddle and began emptying his six-gun. Fargo pressed the rifle trigger as two shots crackled a branch inches from his head. The man straightened in the saddle, his body stiffening. As his horse continued down the incline without him, he seemed to hang in midair for a moment before crashing to the ground. "Damned fool," Fargo muttered as he lowered the rifle and turned back into the trees. Striding to the bush, he kicked it and stepped back. "You can come out now," he said. The girl crawled out from under the bush, dusting grass and dirt from herself as she stood up. Her glance at him showed her smudged face still dark with suspicion and hostility. "You satisfied I wasn't after you?" he asked.

"Why? Because they were after you? What's that prove?" she tossed back. "Maybe they had their own reasons for coming after you. That doesn't mean you weren't looking for me."

"Damn, you're tough to convince," he said and had to admire the logic of her suspicion-wrapped reasoning. He studied her again. Her full, firm supple body had a frightened, skittish quality to it under her belligerent stance. She was plainly in need of help, he decided. "You're coming with me," he said.

"Expected that," she snorted.

"It's not what you're thinking, whatever that is," Fargo said.

"I've some things with me, just past the bush," she said and he nodded, watching as she disappeared into

27

the trees. She re-emerged moments later, carrying a small canvas sack.

"This way. We'll ride," Fargo said and started for the Ovaro. He caught the small, sudden movement, and started to turn just as she smashed the rock into the back of his head. She vanished in an explosion of light and flashes as he felt himself go down. The flashes were replaced by a curtain of grayness and the world disappeared.

Fargo didn't know how long he'd been unconscious when he awoke, slowly sitting up and instantly feeling the throbbing pain in his head. He pulled his eyes open, staring at the ceiling of green leaves, letting thoughts arrange themselves. Anger was the first one to push at him. He'd been entirely too trusting; a plain lapse of judgment. But then, she had been but one more strange thing among all the other strange things that had happened. He rose to his feet, wincing at the dull ache in his head. She was gone, of course. So was his Henry, he saw as he scanned the ground, swearing again. Climbing onto the pinto, he retraced his steps, leaving the hills and crossing the river. He'd go on and find Grange. It was why he was here. Maybe he'd get some answers there.

Following along the Yellow River, he watched the day begin to draw to an end, the lush mountains taking on a soft blue-gray hue. A bighorn sheep leaped from one ledge to another and vanished in the gathering dusk, and a red-tailed hawk soared into the high places. This was a land that never let you forget its wildness—perhaps as a warning. As dusk began to settle down, the river made a sudden sharp turn east. Fargo reined up, his eyes swiveling to the left. The two stands of bigcone-spruce rose up just as the letter had said they would. He turned the horse and went forward at a trot, riding into the wide space bordered by the two forests of spruce.

A frown formed on Fargo's brow. There was plenty of space for a town, but there was none there. He slowed to a halt, dismounted, and began to walk along one edge of the trees, then crossed to the other, circling the wide, flat land. Reality overtook him. There were no buildings, not one broken-down shed, not even an outhouse. This was the place the letter had described, but there was no town, only an empty space and the two big stands of spruce. Nothing else. He realized, almost wryly, that he was not as surprised as he should have been. It was becoming hard to be surprised on this trip.

A town that wasn't there. Seemed almost appropriate, one strange event following another. The dusk began to gather, turning to dark, and Fargo led the pinto into the spruce and found a spot to bed down. He made a small fire as night overtook the land, heated a strip of beef jerky and then stretched out on his bedroll. He let sleep come to him as he wondered about the strange girl hiding in the hills, and why six men had tried to stop him from reaching a town that didn't exist.

The night passed quickly, the buzzing and clicking of night insects serving as a soft lullaby, and he soon awoke with the new day. He found a brook threading through the spruce and washed in the cold, clear water, breakfasting on a wild cherry bush he found. When he finished, he strolled to the edge of the trees and peered out at the open land. He was still staring at the emptiness when a horse and rider appeared, coming closer and finally halting. It was a young woman in a dark shirt and dusty riding britches. Very light blond hair the color of corn silk glistened in the new sun, her skin a delicate pale white. Her hair hung straight, almost to her shoulder, framing a delicate face with a thin, straight nose and nicely molded lips. Eyes, so pale a blue that they seemed almost opaque, scanned the empty space. But a bold jaw gave her face a strength that contrasted with the pale delicacy of the rest of her.

He saw a puzzled look come across her smooth, high brow, the dark tan shirt pulling tightly across full breasts as she crossed her arms. She turned in the saddle and her eyes scanned the empty space, fixed on him as he came forward out of the spruce. "Morning. You looking for Grange, too?" Fargo inquired. "Join the party. I'm expecting a Mr. Baker."

The pale blue eyes found a tiny light that flickered and her full lips edged into a smile. "I'm Mr. Baker," she said. "The B stands for Brenda. You must be Fargo."

"Bull's-eye," he said. "Why use only the initial?"

"Some men don't like working for a woman," Brenda Baker said.

"Wouldn't have bothered me any," Fargo answered.

"I didn't want to take that chance. Wanted to be sure you'd take my offer," she said.

"Well, I'm here, Brenda Baker, but there's no town. You play games about that, too?" Fargo asked.

The furrow deepened on her smooth, high brow. "No, honest I didn't. My cousin Harley wrote me from here a number of times," she said. "I really don't understand any of this. I'm sure this is the right place. He sent me detailed directions."

"You've never been here, I take it," Fargo said.

"No. I've come from Philadelphia. I've never been west of Pennsylvania. But I've heard of ghost towns. Is this what they mean?" Brenda queried.

"No. Ghost towns are towns where the people have all left, not the buildings."

"Why?" she questioned.

"Sometimes a town just never holds itself together and folks leave. Sometimes a new wagon trail passes it by and it just dies off. Sometimes a town lives off one industry, say logging. When that ends, the town shrivels up and withers away. All that's left is empty buildings, prairie rats, and tumbleweed. But the buildings still stand, furniture sometimes still in place, doors hanging open, everything coated in dust, a town only a ghost of what it once was," he explained. "But this is no ghost town. This town doesn't exist—never did, I'd say."

"But it did," Brenda Baker said. "I can show you Harley's letters from here."

"Harley?" Fargo queried.

"Harley Connagher, my cousin. Harley's why I'm here, and also why I sent for you," Brenda said as she dismounted, moving with the practiced smoothness of a good horsewoman. She delved into her saddlebag and pulled out a bundle of envelopes. She handed them to him. "Look at these. They're all stamped from Grange," she said.

He examined the envelopes and saw that they indeed bore the simple, blue-stamped mark put on by the local dispatcher before he dropped the mail into the pouch at the stage. "A few are marked Eakins," Fargo noted.

"Yes, he did send a few from there too." Brenda nodded.

"Well, we know Eakins exists. I rode through it. Some gents there told me there was no such place as Grange. Then they tried to stop me from getting here," Fargo told her.

Her pale blue eyes almost darkened. "That doesn't make any sense," she said.

"Exactly what I've been telling myself," Fargo said. "Hoped you might be able to explain it when we met."

She shrugged helplessly, her corn silk hair shimmering. "I can't. I can't explain any of this," Brenda said, scanning the empty space.

"Maybe I can. I'm thinking Harley gave the wrong directions to the both of us," Fargo said. "Maybe Grange is nowhere near here. That'd explain the gents in Eakins saying it doesn't exist."

"It doesn't explain why they tried to stop you from getting here, though," she threw back, her strong chin tilting upward.

"No, it doesn't," he conceded. "But maybe it was just a wild-goose chase, a mistake on their part."

"Maybe, but my bringing us here was no mistake," she insisted and pulled one of the envelopes open. "Here, read this. It's Cousin Harley's directions in his own handwriting." Fargo scanned the letter and returned it to her, a frown digging into his brow. The instructions were the same as those she had sent him. She hadn't made an error and the letter suddenly took on new proportions. Fargo's eyes swept the empty space. Perhaps it wasn't really empty, he pondered. His world had taught him there was no trail that didn't leave a mark. Had there been a town here? He couldn't dismiss the possibility any longer, couldn't hang his disbelief on a simple error. He began to walk slowly across the wide space to the other side, then went into a crouch as he stepped forward, paralleling the spruce. His eyes narrowed, searching the ground as he traced a straight line.

He halted, letting his fingers move slowly across the soil, pressing harder to dig into the ground. He felt the thin indentation following the line, and came to another that joined it at right angles. He glanced up, and found Brenda beside him. "What are you doing?" she asked.

"What I do best—being a trailsman. It's not so different from following a possum or a badger, or trying to spot a walking leaf. They hide their trails damn well, too," Fargo said and continued to press his fingers into the soil as he moved on. He halted again a few moments later when he felt a difference in the soil under his fingers. New dirt, pressed into the ground to fill tracks that cut deep into the ground. The tracks were made by buildings, by their boards digging into the ground where they stood, he realized and, with excitement welling up inside him, Fargo went on, pressing, scratching, digging. Patterns began to form, taking on the shape of one edge of buildings that had once faced the main street.

A very good job had been done of brushing away surface marks, then putting down new soil to fill in the marks too deep to erase. But to Skye Fargo, soil was not just soil. The ground offered its own language, with newly laid soil having a different texture than old, still holding moisture, its consistency subtly firmer. As he continued to probe and scratch he thanked all the years when nature had taught him to detect the subtleties of soil displaced, replaced, and disguised. He was, he knew, indebted to all the ways wild creatures hid their trails, all their burrowing, covering, and hiding subterfuges he had come to know. Finally, he halted and straightened up, his jaw a tight line.

"Grange did exist here," he told Brenda. "But it was made to disappear. Every building was taken apart. Somebody wiped out the town, made it disappear. It was a very careful and clever job. But even erasing leaves its signs."

"Only to someone such as you, only to the Trailsman," Brenda said, coming to him and rested both hands against his chest. "Thanks for this much."

"Wouldn't call it much. Doesn't explain anything," Fargo demurred.

"In a way, it's everything. Without it, we'd go on thinking there was a mistake. It's what we need to start finding out what happened here. What about my cousin Harley and the others who lived here? Were they made to disappear, too? Or did they run away?"

Fargo saw the girl in the hills flash through his mind. Suddenly, she, too, took on a new dimension. "Maybe I can get a lead on those questions," he said grimly. "But I need some filling in. Why'd you send for me? Why are you here? I think you'd better start at the beginning."

She nodded, her delicately planed face growing grave as he led her to a log at the edge of the spruce. She sat down the bundle of envelopes clutched in one hand. Her almost opaque blue eyes never really darkened, he noticed, but they could take on a troubled grimness. "Maybe I should start by telling you about Harley, and myself," she said.

"Might be a good start," he agreed.

"Harley and I are cousins but he's some twenty years older than I am. We're the only two members of our family left. Though we've lived far apart, we've always stayed in touch. I think we're probably closer than many families who live near each other. I've lived mostly in Philadelphia, worked there as a clerk in a dry-goods store. Harley's always traveled. He's an actor, or, as he prefers to call himself, a thespian."

"Likes the classics?" Fargo asked.

"Yes. Shakespeare, Spenser, Christopher Marlowe, Cervantes." Brenda nodded. "Ever hear of any of them?"

"I've seen Shakespeare. Marlowe, too." Fargo smiled. "Believe it or not."

"I believe it," Brenda said. "You're not the kind to put on airs."

"Thanks," he said. "Let's get back to Harley."

"Harley does other plays, too, and he organized a little troupe of actors to come out here with him. They settled in to put on plays, to bring the theater out to the frontier," Brenda said.

"They picked a pretty wild place." Fargo sniffed. "This is real pioneer country. Folks out here worry about keeping their scalps, working their land, establishing settlements. They don't have the time or the need to watch plays, and the Shoshoni sure aren't going to be a willing audience."

"Harley wouldn't agree with most of that. He always believed that the theater was a part of people, necessary to their lives, a way the ordinary person can shed his own problems and troubles. From the days of the ancient Greek amphitheaters, the people came to plays. Shakespeare's audiences weren't made of kings and queens—mostly it was the common people who flocked in to see his plays. He used to say that the ordinary people of ancient Greece and of medieval days had nothing but hardship and problems. But that didn't keep them from flocking to see plays. He felt it wouldn't stop settlers, pioneers, and farmers, either. He said he'd seen rough mining towns where they flocked to see a touring theater company."

Fargo smiled and had to admit there was perhaps more than a little truth in Cousin Harley's words. "He's still a dedicated dreamer," Fargo said. "But dreamers can convince others. You, for one."

"Yes, and those that came out here with him. I've supported Harley all along, backed him with a number of troupes," Brenda said.

"But from a distance."

"Yes, with my part of the money our Uncle Charles left to us. Uncle Charles wrote a will that said Harley and I had to share anything we made from the money he left us. We agreed and signed the will with him. When he died, it's been that way ever since, with Harley and me sharing anything either of us made out of monies Uncle Charles left us."

"What brought you out here now?" Fargo queried.

"Harley sent for me," she said, extracting some of the envelopes from the bundle and handing them to him. "These are Harley's letters. They'll tell you everything I know." She pushed the top one at him to read first, and he leaned back to take in a bold but flowery script.

Dearest Cousin Brenda . . .

The troupe has been here with me for three months now, but there are sudden, exciting changes. I need you to come here. You've always been the one with a head for business and I need your talents.

I've switched careers. I've become a prospector.

Well, not exactly, but sort of. I haven't lost my love for the theater. It's more like adding another career. We're all excited about it here, so much so we're making plans for building our own theater. Please hurry and come. It will be definitely worth your while.

Love . . . Harley

Brenda took the letter as he finished and gave him another. "Of course, I was intrigued. I started to plan to go visit Harley but I didn't leap into action. Before I could complete my plans I got this letter," she said. Fargo began to read the second letter, penned with the same bold flowery script.

Brenda dearest . . .

I need you to hire a special person for me, for us, a man who makes a living at finding new trails and reading old ones. I'm told that the very best of these is a man named Skye Fargo and he can be reached at a mailing address in Wyoming. I'm noting that down at the bottom of this note.

Pay him to meet you at Grange. Use the directions I sent you last month.

Waiting for you . . . Harley

Fargo's glance dropped to the bottom of the letter, and he saw that Harley Connagher had set down the address of a mail drop set up years ago where he could be contacted. There were others, but this one was perhaps best known. "Now I know how you reached me," he said to Brenda, who nodded and handed him the third letter.

"Harley apparently asked around and someone gave him your name and that address. I wrote to you immediately and sent the advance," Brenda said.

"Then this last letter came." Fargo took the letter and read the few lines aloud.

Brenda dearest . . .
Things have changed, and not for the better. I'm suddenly very afraid for my life. In fact, we are all afraid. It'd terribly important for you to come right away. It's for your good, too. Remember, we share in everything. Hurry, please.
Love . . . Cousin Harley.

"He never gave you any more detail than that?" Fargo asked, handing the letter back.

"No, but after that letter, I took a train as far as I could, switched stagecoaches, and finally reached Yellowstone. I bought a horse and was glad for the riding lessons I'd taken as a little girl back in Philadelphia. I rode hard and here I am, without my cousin Harley in a town that's disappeared. I'm scared, dammit, real scared," Brenda said as she rose, shaking her cornsilk hair. Shafts of pale gold light spun into the air.

"That's easy enough to understand," Fargo said.

The opaque blue eyes turned on him and Brenda's firm chin lifted defiantly. "With me, scared means getting angry. Harley asked me to bring you here. I'll hire you to find out what happened to Harley and this town that used to be. Will you do it? I don't know where else to turn."

"I'm here. You're paying," Fargo said.

Brenda's arms encircled his neck. "That's not enough, not for you," she said.

"Things need explaining here," Fargo admitted. Brenda's lips were soft and fleeting.

"Thank you," she murmured. "You won't be sorry."

"I hope not," he said. "First, I have to try to pick up a trail. What do I do with you, meanwhile? Hide you here in the spruce?"

"Harley had a cabin that can't be far from here," Brenda said.

"How do you know that?" Fargo asked.

"He wrote me about it sometime ago, describing it to me. He said they used it when they needed a quiet space for rehearsal," Brenda explained. "But he didn't tell me exactly where it was."

"What did he tell you?"

"It was deep in a forest, east from town," Brenda said.

Fargo thought aloud for a moment. "Well, we know where town was. This spruce forest ought to be east of it, I'd guess. Let's ride," he said. Brenda came alongside him as he slowly guided the horse through the spruce. She rode only reasonably well, Fargo noted, her body held too stiffly. But it kept her breasts straining against the tan shirt. He smiled inwardly, glad for small favors. They had ridden some twenty minutes when the trees began to thin. The cabin came into sight minutes afterward, larger than he had expected. Fargo drew to a halt, dismounted, and went into the cabin. He found a room with a table and a hearth, three chairs, and a hooked rug on the floor. Pine shelves held rows of books. Plays, he saw at a quick glance, some loosely bound in manuscript form.

A second room held two cots and a small dresser, and he returned to the front room to see Brenda there. "This will do fine," he said. "It's hidden away. Stay here till I get back."

"When will that be?" she queried.

"Before night, I hope. But you stay here and wait," he said and her arms went around him again.

"Be careful. You're suddenly very important to me. I know that sounds selfish," Brenda said.

"I'll make allowances," he said and saw a tiny light deep in her azure eyes. She remained in the doorway as he climbed onto the Ovaro and rode away. He thought back to the handsome Shoshoni girl, about the strange bargain he had made with her father, of the men who had tried to stop him from reaching Grange, and of a town that had been literally removed from existence. The strange and the unexpected kept coming, Fargo mused, now thinking about corn silk hair and pale, pale blue eyes. Only now it was getting more interesting.

3

Fargo retraced his steps, crossing the river's yellow-tinged water and climbing into the hills of hackberry and cottonwoods. He halted where he had let the girl get away and swore again at his carelessness. Dismounting, he carefully scanned the forest floor until he picked up her footprints. He trailed the prints, seeing that she had stayed on foot. Fargo grunted in surprise—he'd expected she would change to a horse somewhere. Her prints were easy enough to follow. She'd made no effort to conceal her tracks. She was either too bent on fleeing or too confident that her tracks wouldn't be picked up, he told himself when suddenly her prints disappeared.

Fargo halted, finding himself staring at a thick growth of shrubs and bushes, the scruffy foliage of shadscale, thick coralberry, and even denser clusters of blue elderberry shrubs. A virtual wall of thick greenery faced him and he cautiously pushed through to see the hillside had become a collection of caves, with at least three of them directly in front of him. Each cave entrance was shielded by the thick growths of brush and shrub, and it was here that the girl's footprints had vanished. She had grown careful and clever, he half smiled, obviously banking on nature's aid in turning back searchers. Not only did the caves present a formidable challenge, she had taken now to stepping only where her footprints didn't show, on patches of broad leaves on the forest floor, or rocks and logs, and through little streams that trickled through the hills.

Few who followed this far would have been able to follow further, their search reduced to aimless chance. But Fargo was not the ordinary searcher. He knelt down, his eyes searching the foliage almost leaf by leaf. It took him longer than he wanted but finally he spotted the signs he sought—the places where leaves were bruised, their ends turned in, small branches broken off. This was where she had pushed her way through the thick foliage and he saw the path become a straight line into the center cave. He walked through the cave's opening and found it honeycombed with passages that led deeper into the darkness. Her footprints showed that she had traveled down each passage, and Fargo swore softly as he knelt down at the first set.

He pressed his fingers into the thin topsoil, then went onto the next passage and the next, finally allowing a thin smile as his fingers found prints that were still fresh and moist. He rose, and cautiously followed the trail down the passageway. As he moved deeper, the light began to fade, but then suddenly brightened as the glow of a small candle cast thin light further down the passage. When Fargo reached it, he saw the passage widen to become another, smaller cave. The girl was there, sitting on a torn piece of blanket. Fargo scanned the cave and saw a tin pot, a small bundle of clothes, a hunting knife on the ground, and a tin plate holding what were obviously a collection of old, bleached bones. Probably wildfowl or rabbit, he guessed. He also saw his rifle leaning against one wall.

Returning his eyes to the girl, he saw a depressed piece of stone beside her, filled with water. As he watched, she began to take off her torn shirt, letting it fall to one side as she dipped a piece of cloth into the water. She then began to wash the dirt from herself, starting with her face. He took in her nice rounded shoulders, her breasts, though a little on the small side, were nicely curved, dark pink tips centered on lighter pink circles. They fitted her smallish ribcage and neat, trim little body. She reached down to push the torn jeans from her legs, and he saw her flat abdomen with just the hint of a curve to it, a surprisingly full little V-shaped nap, and smooth-skinned thighs that were just covered with enough muscle to avoid being thin.

She continued to wash and his eyes went to her face. No longer smudged with dirt, he saw she had a pretty face with small but even features, a short nose, and full lips, round cheeks, and wavy, dark brown hair almost matching the brown of her eyes. She dried herself off with a towel and rose to her feet, and Fargo nodded appreciatively at the tight compact loveliness of her figure, more sweet than seductive. He waited until she had pulled her clothes back on before he moved forward, drawing his gun. He'd no thoughts of using it on her but she lived in fear and distrust. She'd already proved that. He needed an instant of surprise, something to freeze her own quick reactions.

He crept another few paces, took careful aim, and fired. The plate of old bones leaped into the air and she screamed in surprise and fright, her body tightening. "I could miss next time," Fargo said as he stepped forward. She stared at him, her brown eyes wide as he moved past her, taking the Henry from the wall and holstering the Colt. Her eyes narrowed at him.

"How long have you been there?" she asked.

"Long enough," he said blandly, seeing her cheeks grow red. Her lips tightened and he saw the resignation slide across her face.

"All right, you've found me. Took you long enough," she spat.

"Only a few hours," he said.

"You've been hunting for me for weeks," she said.

"No, you're all wrong there. You've been wrong about me from the start, damnit," Fargo snapped. "You've a name?" he asked.

"Hazel Atwood," she said and her eyes narrowed at him, studying him with fear, suspicion, and uncertainty. "If you weren't looking for me, what were you doing up here?" she asked.

"On my way to find a town called Grange," he said and saw surprise leap into her face. "What do you know about Grange?" he pressed quickly. She pulled the shock from her face and stared back at him blankly. "It's time you started talking, Hazel. What happened to Grange?"

"What do you mean, what happened to it?" She frowned.

"It's gone," he said.

"Gone?" She frowned.

"Disappeared. Vanished. No more," Fargo said. "I want to know what happened. You lived there. That's becoming pretty damn plain."

Hazel Atwood pushed to her feet, surprise wreathing her face, her lips parted. "Oh, my God." She breathed.

"Talk to me, girl," Fargo said. She swayed, starting to collapse and he caught her in his arms, holding her up.

"I'm sorry. I haven't eaten in days," she murmured, clinging to him.

"We can fix that," he said, keeping his arm around her as he walked her from the cave to where he had left the Ovaro. He fished a strip of beef jerky from his saddlebag and let her fold herself on the ground as she devoured the food.

"Thank you," Hazel said when she finished, her brown eyes taking on a new softness as they studied him. "It seems I was wrong about you. I'm glad I missed that shot," she said, her hand coming to rest on his.

"That makes two of us," Fargo said and settled down beside her. "Now tell me whatever you know about Grange."

"It was our town. At least Harley always called it that. He named us the Grange Players," Hazel said.

"Us?"

"I was one of the troupe. There were ten of us, including Harley," she said. "You say the whole town is gone?"

"All of it, disappeared," Fargo told her.

"It was there when they came through. We were all there," Hazel said.

"When who came through?"

"The riders. There must have been thirty of them. First they took all of us who were part of the troupe," Hazel said. "Then they started shooting the other people in town, the storekeepers, the townspeople, even

Harry Giddins, the town drunk. It was terrible." Her voice broke and she shuddered. He held her for a moment, her softness pressing into him as she clung on to his biceps. "Then they took the rest of us prisoner, everybody who was part of the troupe."

"How'd you get away?" he asked.

"Luck. I saw a chance and ran. They looked but never found me," Hazel said. "They kept searching for me for the next two weeks. But Grange was there when I got away. I stole back the next night and got a few of my things."

"It's not there anymore. It was wiped away. I hoped you'd have some answers for that," Fargo said.

"I don't," she said, the shock still in her face.

Fargo let thoughts churn inside him as he frowned into space. "You've told me a few things I need to sort out. But first, I'm taking you somewhere better than this," he said.

She leaned against him, her hands on his chest. "I'd appreciate that," she said, then lifted her head and pressed her lips to his, a sweet, light touch. "Thank you." She murmured.

"You want to take anything?" Fargo asked.

"A few clothes. That's all I have," she said, then hurried into the cave and returned with a bundle under one arm. She sat the saddle in front of him and he felt the warmness of her round little rear against him. The day was drawing to a close as he rode from the concealed bank of caves and into the forest. Dusk had begun to settle when he reached the two spruce forests where the town had been. "My God, it's gone . . . just gone!" Hazel gasped. "Why did they wipe out the town?"

"I wish I could answer that," Fargo said.

"They took Harley and the troupe as prisoners. Why just us?" Hazel wondered aloud.

"I'm still wrestling with that," Fargo said as he kept moving through the spruce. It was nearly dark when he reached the cabin, where a candle glowed from inside. Brenda appeared at the door with a rifle in hand, which she lowered when she saw Fargo dismount with Hazel. He led Hazel into the cabin and saw Brenda's pale blue eyes survey her. "Hazel Atwood," he introduced. "Found her hiding out on the hills. She escaped from Grange." He quickly told Brenda what Hazel had said about the attack by the thirty riders. "Hazel was part of your cousin Harley's troupe," he finished.

Brenda's eyebrows lifted but her pale blue orbs held a wariness as she eyed Hazel. "What did you do in the troupe?" she asked.

"I was one of the actresses," Hazel said.

"What have you played?" Brenda pushed at her.

"Viola in *Twelfth Night,* Titiana in *A Midsummer Night's Dream,* Luciana in *The Comedy of Errors,*" Hazel said. "You always this suspicious?"

"The way things have been going, I suspect everything," Brenda said. "You could have just been on the run and handed Fargo a convenient story."

"Well, I didn't." Hazel bristled.

"Your answers were good enough," Brenda said.

"Thanks," Hazel said, an edge of sarcasm in her voice. "I'm very grateful to Fargo."

"I imagine you are," Brenda said coolly.

"Hazel's the only piece we have to this puzzle," Fargo said.

"I wish I had more to tell you, Fargo," Hazel said.

"You may know more than you realize," Fargo told

her. "A few things are taking on new meanings. Wiping out Grange is one of them. Somebody wanted to be sure nobody would ever go there looking, digging and poking around, asking about it, finding anything about anyone that ever lived there. Why, is question one. Why were you and the rest of the troupe taken alive? That's question two. Can you make any connection?"

"No," Hazel said. "Harley's the only one who might. He's been very worried about something lately, but he never told us what."

"That ties in with his last letter," Brenda said.

"That's right," Fargo said. "That leaves question three. What's happened to Harley Connagher and the rest of the troupe?"

"Do you think they've been killed, too?" Hazel asked in alarm.

"Can't be sure, but I'm thinking no," Fargo said.

"Why?" Brenda questioned.

"There had to be a reason they weren't killed along with the others. I'm hoping that reason is still keeping them alive," he said. "Let me have another look at those letters from Harley. Maybe there's a clue in there someplace."

Brenda brought out the letters, and he read them through twice, finally handing them back to her. "Find anything?" she questioned.

"No, except that one reference to having become a prospector and he made that into a half joke. But maybe that fits in someplace. Then again, maybe not," Fargo said.

"It fits," Hazel said. "Somehow, someway. I know he'd become very friendly with an old prospector."

"Who?" Brenda cut in.

"He never mentioned a name," Hazel said.

"Did you recognize any of the men who hit Grange?" Fargo questioned, and she shook her head no. "I'll start with what we have, little as it is," he said.

"Such as?" Brenda put in.

"The six men who tried to stop me from looking for Grange. I think they worked for Sam Eakins. Maybe a coincidence. Maybe not. But first, I want you two safe here, holed up and out of sight. I'll stock you up on food and get some new clothes for you, Hazel," he said with a glance at the darkness outside. "Meanwhile, we could all use some sleep. There are two cots, one for each of you."

"What about you?" Hazel asked.

"I've my bedroll," Fargo said.

Hazel linked her arm in his. "No need for that. You can share my cot," she said.

"You won't be sharing anything with him," Brenda cut in sharply and stepped to the door. "A word with you," she said to Fargo and he followed her outside. Her pale blue eyes took on a fierce intensity. "You're here to find out what happened to Harley and the others, not to get involved in distractions," she said icily. "I hired you. I'm paying you. Things will be my way."

"She was just being hospitable," he said.

"Bullshit. You're the only one she has to turn to. I'll not have you making her a concern of yours," Brenda snapped.

"She's our only connection to what's happened. It's strictly business," Fargo said.

"Then sleeping alone will help keep it that way," Brenda returned tartly.

"Sharing a cot doesn't mean screwing, honey," Fargo said. "Or maybe that never occurred to you."

"I want to make sure," she said stiffly.

"As you said, it's your nickel so it's your call. For now," he answered. "Besides, I'm flattered."

"Why?" Brenda frowned.

"You being so bothered I might sleep with her," Fargo said.

"That's got nothing to do with it," she flung back, but he was already striding into the cabin. Inside, Hazel waited, her eyes studying him as he appeared.

"I'll be using my bedroll," he said. Her brows lifted as a wry smile edged her lips.

"Another surprise," she commented. "Didn't see you as the kind to back down."

"There's a time to back down and a time not to back down," Fargo said.

"What makes the difference, how you feel?" She sniffed.

"What's right. Keeping your agreements. You've a sharp little tongue," he said.

"I don't like her," Hazel muttered.

"She's got the same interests as you—finding Harley," Fargo reminded her.

"The same, but different," she said.

"Get some sleep," he said and walked out of the cabin. He met Brenda just as she was starting to enter, glaring at him.

"You can sleep with her whenever you want, just not on my time," she said tightly.

"You're still bothered aren't you?" He laughed.

"Damn you," he heard her hiss as he strode away. When he reached the Ovaro, he took down his bedroll, stretched out in the spruce, and let sleep quickly overtake him. When morning came, he used his canteen to wash up. The cabin was still silent and asleep when he rode away. He set a brisk pace through the trees, having decided to pick up the supplies. He put off a meeting with Sam Eakins until he had stocked up the cabin. He knew the meeting would be a fishing expedition and was prepared to move carefully. But he rode on confidently, plans forming in his mind. He circumvented the town so he could come in from the other side, where he'd noted most of the stores were clustered. He was passing a few of the farms and homes in the low hills when his plans suddenly came apart, much like a torn scarf frays and shreds at the edges.

His eyes were sweeping the high hills, an automatic practice, when he spied the first line of near-naked riders. Immediately, his glance shifted, his eyes narrowing, and he picked up the second line of bucks on horseback. He found the third group after a few moments more. Edging into the cottonwoods and Gambel oak, he steered the pinto upward, carefully staying in the trees. When he was close enough to the third line of riders, he slowed and watched as the Indians formed a long half circle in the high hills that let them look down on the land below. He noted the armbands on a few of the near-naked riders. Shoshoni, he muttered silently.

Some of their ponies wore warpaint, he noticed grimly. They were plainly a line of scouts, positioning themselves to survey the lower land from every angle, watching every movement, making note of every detail. They wouldn't miss anything, he knew, taking in anything that walked, crawled, or flew. He cursed silently as his thoughts went to Jed Hopper and the homes and farms clustered on the low hills. Slowly, he backed the Ovaro down the cottonwoods, then turned and rode back to the low hills. As he neared Jed Hopper's farm and the half circle of homes on the hillside, he found himself cursing angrily and wasn't certain at whom.

Jed Hopper and his family, and those around him, had no clue to the storm gathering above them. Though the riders he had seen were scouts, what the army would call their reconnaissance patrol, fury would come another day. The low hills and houses drew closer and he saw Jed Hopper's red beard as the man worked beside a wagon, his two boys nearby. Fargo steered the pinto toward the house and heard himself cursing again. He had his own obligations, Fargo told himself. He had his own mystery to unravel. He wasn't being paid to save the world. Brenda had made it very clear what he was being paid to do. These people had set down roots in this wild, untamed land. They should have been prepared to defend themselves properly. But then, fools and dreamers were seldom prepared. They were too busy trusting in their dreams.

But he wasn't their guardian angel, he told himself. They weren't his mission. He had other concerns, perhaps with lives also waiting to be saved. Time was crucial to Harley Connagher and the others. Their lives hung on how quickly he got to them and found out had happened. Or perhaps it was already too late for Harley and his troupe. *Perhaps*. The word rode up, blazing through him. It grew, taking on its own meaning and power until it became a kind of command. With Harley and the others, he was chasing a question mark. Everything was perhaps. But there was no question as to what would happen here, Fargo thought as he drew up before Jed Hopper. And no choice, either, he knew, but not without bitterness. Here there was only time, he knew, and precious little of it. "Morning, Fargo," Jed Hopper called out as his wife appeared, a rake in her hand, a plain, gray cotton dress over her small frame. "Glad to see you've stayed on," the man said.

"Remember the question I asked you last time?" Fargo said.

"About the Shoshoni?"

"That's right. I'm not asking this time. I'm telling. They're going to hit you, and everybody on this hill," Fargo said. "I'd guess tomorrow morning."

The man frowned and Fargo saw his wife step forward, her face instantly drawn in fright. "How do you know that?" Jed Hopper queried.

"I know the Shoshoni. I know their ways. Their advance scouts are watching you now, high in the hills," Fargo said. The man's eyes instantly scanned the high hills behind him. "Don't bother trying to see them. You won't. Just take my word for it," Fargo said.

The man turned back to Fargo. "I told you how we'd be surprising them," he said. "I'll alert the others."

"Your plan won't work. They already know what you figure to do," Fargo said. "You won't be able to defend a single house. They won't let you. They'll hit every one of you at once."

Jed Hopper frowned, turning Fargo's words in his mind. "You sound sure of it," he muttered.

"I am," Fargo said.

"Listen to the man," Jed's wife pleaded. "He's got no reason to tell us anything but the truth."

The man drew a deep sigh. "What can we do?" he asked.

"Get the others together. When night falls, dig a trench from in front of the last house and down along the others. Dig it deep enough for everybody to stay in it. They've already marked the position of your houses. They'll come charging at each one. They won't even see your ditch at first. You lay down your fire from the trench. That way, you'll be able to hit them hard."

"And we'll be down where they can't really get clean shots at us," the man said, excitement seizing his voice.

"Bull's-eye," Fargo said. "Do it right and you can win it. It's your only chance. Staying holed up in your houses will be suicide."

"I'll start telling the others," the man said.

"No digging till after dark. They'll be back in their camp by then," Fargo warned.

"You'll be fighting with us, of course, right Fargo?" Jed Hopper said, and Fargo winced inside. The man's words had struck at the core of the personal dilemma he faced. The Shoshoni were watching him talk to Jed Hopper. That wouldn't bother them. They'd see that as ordinary. But if they saw him taking part in the battle, killing Shoshoni, it would mean the end of the pact their chief had made with him. He didn't want that, Fargo reminded himself. While he was here in Shoshoni country, he wanted the protection that pact afforded him. Somehow, he'd not stopped feeling it might be important sometime, in someway. His eyes went to Jed Hopper and knew that if he told the man about the Shoshoni pact, the man would stop believing him. He didn't want that, either. Jed Hopper was frowning at him. "I didn't get your answer," the man said.

"I'll be with you but you won't see me," he said and the man's frown deepened. "I'll be back in the trees. You'll need somebody to pick off the ones who get through to you."

"You know best," Hopper said.

"I'll be back during the night," Fargo said, then turned the pinto and rode away. He rode toward Eakins with his mouth a tight, grim line. His plan wouldn't save all of them. Nothing could do that. But it would save most of them from being wiped out trying to fight the Shoshoni the wrong way. He'd help them as best he could, he promised himself, knowing he'd be playing a dangerous game. When he reached Eakins from the far end of town he found the general store and filled a sack with tinned food and some utensils, and added a bag of potatoes. He then found clothes he guessed would fit Hazel. "You know where I'd find a town called Grange?" he asked the storekeeper, a thin-faced man.

"Sorry," the storekeeper said quickly. "There are a lot of new towns springing up. I don't know most of them." Fargo's eyes watched the man closely but he could catch nothing in the thin face that told him anything.

"Seems to me that Sam Eakins pretty much owns this town," Fargo remarked casually. "His name's on damn near everything."

"You could say that," the storekeeper said evenly. Fargo returned a polite nod and hurried out to the pinto. He circled back from town the way he had come, and it was dusk by the time he reached the cabin.

"You took a lot longer than I expected," Brenda said as Hazel looked on.

"Unexpected detour," he said, tossing Hazel the clothes. She hurried into the other room with them.

"You meet with Sam Eakins?" Brenda asked.

"No," he said.

"What about tonight?" she pressed.

"I'll be busy," he said, swearing inwardly as he told her what he was going to do.

"You can't. You have to find out what's happened to Harley. The damn settlers will have to fend for themselves."

"You're all heart, Brenda," Fargo said.

"I've heart. I've also got priorities," she snapped.

"So do I, and mine are to stop a lot of men, women, and children from being killed come morning," he said.

She threw a glare at him and her voice was tight when she answered. "It's not fair," she said truculently.

"Didn't say it was fair. Just said it was right," he answered and she didn't reply. Hazel appeared then, clad in the new jeans and shirt he had bought.

"You've a good eye, Fargo. Everything fits perfectly," she said happily. Her smile faded as she felt the tension in the room. "What is it?" she asked.

"There'll be a delay in finding out about Harley and the others," he said and quickly told her the rest. "Brenda doesn't agree with my priorities. You're welcome to join her," he said.

Hazel took a moment to answer. "You do whatever you feel you have to do," she said finally.

"Isn't that noble." Brenda sniffed.

"Isn't that bitchy," Hazel shot back.

Brenda ignored her, keeping her eyes on Fargo. "You better come back," she muttered.

"I plan to," he said, then turned and left the room. Night had fallen, and he rode the pinto through the dark forest, reaching the trees beyond Eakins when the moon rose high enough to shed light. The pale white sphere was nearing the midnight sky when Fargo finally reached the low hills beyond Eakins. The houses were dark but Fargo saw that the tunnel had been dug, and he found Jed Hooper working beside three other men. Hopper called out as he rode to a halt. Others quickly came.

"Been waiting for you," Hopper said. "This what you wanted us to do?"

"It's good enough," Fargo said. "Now lay some planks and logs over the top. Pull up some of your lettuce and squash and lay them over the planks. Throw in some shrubs. When the Shoshoni come they'll just see a new row of plantings. When they come charging the houses, you stay low. Hold your fire until they're near you, then let fly with everything you have. Don't pick targets. Lay down one barrage after another and keep firing."

Hopper turned to the others. "You heard the man. Get the planks and the rest of what we'll need." As they hurried away, he turned his attention back to Fargo. "Got any ideas when they'll hit?" he questioned.

"Be ready when dawn comes up," Fargo said. "I'll see you when it's over. Good luck." He turned the pinto and rode away, turning the horse up to the top of the hills where the forest grew thick with cottonwoods and hackberry. He sat down and leaned back against the deeply furrowed bark of an old cotton-wood, letting his eyes roam across the hills below. There was only the waiting, now, and Fargo found his thoughts turning to a town that no longer existed, a ghost town in the real sense of the word. One fact kept pushing itself at him. Harley Connagher and his little troupe had been the only ones taken alive. Why? Were they more than just traveling players? Perhaps a little more probing with Hazel might be in order, he pondered.

He continued to speculate as the hours drifted away, letting himself doze. But he was fully awake when the first pink fingers of dawn touched the sky. He was scanning the high hills, paused for a quick glance down at the trench below, and allowed a grunt of satisfaction. They had done a good job of laying the lettuce, shrubs, and vegetables over the planks. He returned his eyes to the high hills. A tingling crept over his body and he knew what it meant. Danger was closing in, his feral instincts providing the inner warning ordinary senses failed to supply. He took down the big Henry, cradling it in one arm. It wouldn't be a long wait, he was certain.

4

It was as if the trees and flowers were suddenly spewing forth seeds. Only the seeds were charging horsemen bursting from the foliage in an explosion of war cries. The Shoshoni were already at a full gallop as they charged into the open and down the hillside. Fargo saw a double line of them, perhaps fifty in all, he guessed, and as he expected, they attacked every house at once. Using both rifle fire and arrows, they swept down to attack, circling around to come at the houses from the front. They were nearing the disguised trench, ignoring it in their haste to pour firepower into the houses, when the ditch erupted in a hail of gunfire.

Fargo rose, stepped to the edge of the trees, and saw that the first barrage from the trench had been effective, though not devastating. Almost a dozen Shoshoni fell from their ponies, and the second barrage took down another eight. Taken completely by surprise, the Indians reined up, milling around for a moment before turning to race away. Their confusion cost them another six braves. But their second line of attackers had hardly been touched, Fargo saw, and the Shoshoni adjusted tactics quickly, splitting the second line of braves to come at the trench from both ends.

They converged on the ditch not only from each end but from both sides, and he saw some of the attackers drop from their horses to fight on foot, where they could dart in closer.

Some of the braves on foot came close enough to fire down into the trench while the horsemen poured rifle fire into the long furrow. Fargo raised the Henry and fired, picking off three of the Shoshoni who had gotten close to the tunnel, then he took down a fourth. But he saw that five braves halted their ponies, peering up into the trees where his shots had come from. He held his fire as they continued to scan the trees as another three Shoshoni leaped down into the far end of the trench. They emerged seconds later pulling two women with them. Fargo cursed as the five on their ponies still searched the trees. He didn't want them charging up after him. They had all seen him at the camp that day with Awenita and her father. It would only take one to recognize him, and his pact with the chief would be shattered.

But the others were dragging the two women to their ponies. "Shit," Fargo swore aloud. "So much for the pact." He raised the big Henry, fired off a trio of shots, and the three Shoshoni dragging the women fell as one. But the shots let the five on their ponies pinpoint the source of his fire. They sent their ponies into an instant gallop up the hill toward him. Fargo drew back, turned, and ran some dozen yards, where he flung himself into a thick cluster of five-foot tall ironweed. He lay prone, and peered through the strong stems and the curtain of leaves. The Indians came into sight, separating as they began to search through the trees. They might just overlook him, Fargo thought.

The ironweed was tall and dense and he let himself indulge in hope.

But suddenly, one of the Shoshoni halted, raised his head, and drew the air in with a deep breath, then moved his horse toward his position. The others started to follow at once and Fargo swore silently. He hadn't moved. The Indian hadn't spotted any motion in the ironweed. But like every Shoshoni, the Indian had relied as much on his nose as his eyes and ears. He had picked up the smell of saddle leather on Fargo's clothes and the scent of perspiration. Fargo gathered his muscles. He couldn't just lie there, he knew. The Shoshoni would zero in on him, all pouring shots or arrows into the ironweed. His finger on the trigger of the rifle, Fargo flung himself sideways, hearing the shots slam into the ground where he just was. He came up on his stomach and fired at the nearest Indian. The brave's midsection exploded in a shower of scarlet as he flew from his pony.

Fargo shifted the rifle and fired again, and the next Shoshoni clutched at his shoulder as he toppled from his mount. The big Henry barked again and a third brave screamed, then fell from his mount and lay still. The fourth Shoshoni sprayed fire and Fargo had to roll again, coming up beside the trunk of an old hackberry as bullets thudded into the tree inches from his head. Fargo fired two shots, almost from the hip, and the brave seemed to collapse inward before he slid backward from his pony. The last of the Shoshoni appeared to his left, staring at him through the leaves. Fargo saw recognition and surprise in the man's eyes, and then the Indian was firing. Fargo flung himself backward, feeling the wood chips from the tree hit him as bullets slammed into the bark.

Fargo was now on his back, scuttling for safety behind another tree trunk when he saw the Shoshoni turn and start to race away. Fargo pushed himself up and fired, but the shot went wide. He fired again, much too fast, and the Shoshoni kept going. On his feet, Fargo cursed as he ran after the disappearing Indian. The Shoshoni would race back to his camp, he knew. The pact with the chief was over, Fargo grimaced and he trotted to where he had left the Ovaro hidden in the trees. He had just reached the horse when he heard the single shot ring out and he turned to run toward the sound. He skidded to a halt as he saw Jed Hopper and two other men standing over the slain Shoshoni on the ground. "Saw them come up here after you," Jed Hopper said. "We got him racing back. Thought they'd done you in."

"No. Close, but no such luck," Fargo said. "What about the others?"

"They broke off and ran away," Jed Hopper said. Fargo glanced down at the dead Shoshoni. He'd not be carrying tales back to camp. The pact with Wamblee was still in effect. Gratitude pushed at Fargo. Premonitions, inner voices, vague signs—they were never his thing. Yet from the beginning he'd found himself feeling he'd need something extra in this wild Shoshoni country. The ghost town only added to it. Jed Hopper's voice cut into his thoughts.

"We've plenty wounded but nobody killed, thanks to you, Fargo," the man said as the others offered their thanks. Fargo led the Ovaro down to where everyone had gathered outside the trench, many being bandaged. "Will they be back?" Jed Hopper asked.

"Someday. But you'll have time to build yourselves a real blockhouse, the kind the settlers in Kentucky put up. They saved their communities. So did the first settlers in the plains country," Fargo said.

Amy Hopper stepped forward, her two youngsters with her. "Will you be visiting us, Fargo, to give us pointers?" she asked.

"Maybe," he said, keeping his voice casual. "I'm here looking for a town called Grange. Can't seem to find it. Any of you know it?" he asked. He saw the quick, furtive exchange of glances between the others.

"Can't say I do," Jed Hopper said.

"Me neither," another man said.

One of Jed Hopper's youngsters cut in. "But you've all . . ." he began when his father cut him off.

"No one spoke to you, Paul," Hopper said sharply, and the boy fell silent.

Fargo allowed a half smile. "Out of the mouths of babes?" he said. Jed Hopper and the others shuffled uncomfortably.

"We're sorry, Fargo, but you've got to understand," the man said.

"Sam Eakins own the mortgage on your farm, huh, Jed?" Fargo asked.

"And everybody else's mortgage," the man said.

"We're also into him for feed bills, supplies—just about everything," another man put in, shrugging helplessly. He didn't need to press any further. They had been ordered to forget that Grange had ever existed. They were obligated to obey, their own kind of prisoner, free men who weren't free. But one thing had become clear. Sam Eakins was no longer someone to check out. He was the key figure behind all this, and an increasingly ominous one. Fargo turned and pulled himself onto the Ovaro.

"I'll try to stop by," he said.

"We'd all like that," Jed Hopper called after him as Fargo rode on with a wave. Not hurrying, Fargo kept the horse at a slow trot. He wanted time to focus his thoughts on a man he'd never met. If Sam Eakins had made Grange, and everyone in it, disappear, he had to either be afraid of something or protecting something. Maybe both. There'd be no clever way of approaching him. A man who'd made a town vanish would be too alert to any subtle questions. But maybe directness could be its own weapon, Fargo pondered. Maybe making Sam Eakins more afraid and nervous might shake him up. It wouldn't be the first time nervousness and fear had made a man make mistakes. Maybe that was the only way to shake the real answers loose, Fargo decided. It'd be the dangerous way, he knew, but he couldn't come up with anything better. As he rode into town, he knew the real answers still waited.

What was important enough to erase a town out of existence? Why were Harley Connagher and his little troupe of players held apart? As he slowly made his way through town, Fargo passed the Eakins Pleasure Palace, seeing that it was busy though the night was still hours away. Main Street was crowded with Owensboro farm wagons, a few light-bodied fruit-rack wagons, a few Conestogas, and an assortment of buckboards and surreys. News of the Shoshoni attack hadn't reached the town yet, but Fargo wondered how much effect it would have. Some would think again about putting down roots in the territory, he was sure. But others would trust in prayers, luck, or complacency. He rode on through town until he came to Sam Eakins's place and halted to scan the three long bunkhouses he'd seen before. Inside the big corral and the even larger open yard, Fargo saw the number of hands had increased.

He made a quick count, coming up with sixty men. A second wagon had been drawn up behind the first, also loaded with mining tools, including a hopper and cradle. Another twenty men lounged near the wagons, older men with the worn, weathered hands of prospectors. Fargo steered the pinto around the barn and corral toward the imposing house beyond. He drew up before a heavy oak door inside a columned porchway. An iron bell hung suspended from a carved, wrought-iron holder attached to the door. A man carrying a rifle appeared as he dismounted. "Come to see Sam Eakins," Fargo announced.

"What's your business, stranger?" the man said, plainly a guard.

"I'm not sure." Fargo smiled.

The guard's face was wary. "That's not much of an answer, mister," he said.

"It's the best I can do," Fargo said.

"It's not good enough. Hit the saddle," the man said, his voice hardening.

"Just call your boss," Fargo said.

"I'm not going to tell you twice," the guard said. "Get moving."

Fargo drew a deep sigh. It had been a long night and an even longer day. "I'll just have to ring that bell myself," he said. The guard frowned at him, opening his mouth to answer. Fargo drew and fired, his shot and the clang of the bell sounding at once. The guard's jaw dropped in astonishment and his face paled. "Don't make me ring your bell," Fargo said.

"What the hell's going on?" a voice boomed as the door flew open and a large, burly man stormed from the house, wearing a silk shirt partially covered by a flowered silk vest. Fargo took in the man's barrel chest, his salt-and-pepper hair, and his heavy face and prominent nose.

"He did it, Mr. Eakins," the guard said quickly.

"Want to talk to you," Fargo said mildly.

"You got a funny way of saying so." Sam Eakins frowned.

"Your man was giving me a hard time." Fargo shrugged as he holstered the Colt. Eakins shot a hard glance at his guard.

"Never saw shootin' like that," the guard said apologetically.

Eakins threw him a contemptuous snort and motioned to Fargo. "Come inside," he said and Fargo followed the burly man into the well-furnished house, making his way into a living room of heavy, comfortable furniture. "Who the hell are you?" Eakins tossed at him.

"Name's Fargo."

"What do you do beside's shooting at doorbells?" Eakins asked.

"All kinds of things. Some call me the Trailsman," Fargo said.

"What do you want to talk to me about, Trailsman?" Sam Eakins asked.

"A town I can't find. You're a big man around here. Got a town with your name on it. Figured you'd know what happened to a place called Grange," Fargo said. He watched the man's heavy face closely, but caught no change in its expression of suspicion.

"No such town around here," Eakins said.

"Not now," Fargo said.

"What's that supposed to mean?" Eakins thrust at him.

"It means that Grange was here, but it's disappeared."

Eakins stared back and Fargo had to admire the man's composure. "You've been eating loco weed," Eakins said calmly.

"No, I've been doing what I do best—reading signs and finding trails. I found a place where a town once stood, and doesn't anymore," Fargo said.

"You read wrong," Eakins said.

"I don't read signs wrong," Fargo said. "You know why Grange disappeared?"

"I told you, I never heard of it. Nobody around here has," Eakins said, a hint of smugness creeping into his tone. "What's so important to you about this town?" he questioned.

"Had a job promised me," Fargo said. "Don't like to lose a job. Never lost one before. Never lost a town, either."

"Can't help you, Fargo. Somebody gave you the wrong directions," Sam Eakins said, becoming almost affable. "Where are you staying, in case I hear anything. I'll ask around."

Fargo's smile was chiding and he enjoyed watching the man's eyes harden. "In and around. I'll check back with you," Fargo said.

"Do that. But you're wasting your time," Eakins said. Fargo held his smile as he walked from the house and climbed onto the pinto. The guard watched him ride off with grudging respect, and Fargo sent the horse toward town. It was done, he reflected grimly. He'd torn open pretense, made it clear he knew Grange had been wiped away. More importantly, that he was going to keep digging for reasons. Eakins couldn't ignore that. He'd have to make a move, perhaps more than one. Fargo's lips set into a tight line as he rode. He'd set sudden death into motion, aimed right at him. But he hoped he'd also done what he really wanted to accomplish, triggering Eakins into making a mistake.

As for himself, Fargo knew he'd now have to watch his every moment. Dusk was starting to settle over the town when he rode down Main Street. He was halfway through town when, in the last slanting rays of the sun, he caught the flash of corn silk hair near the general store. "Shit," he swore as he yanked the horse to a halt, swung from the saddle, and confronted the slender figure with the package under one arm. "What the hell are you doing here in town?" he hissed, barely controlling the desire to shout the words. "You out of your mind?"

She turned her pale blue eyes on him with unruffled calm. "Not at all. I decided to snoop around on my own," she said.

"You hired me for that," he threw back.

"I got tired of waiting for you and your good deeds," she sniffed.

"You asking to disappear like Grange?" he pushed at her.

"No. Sam Eakins doesn't know me. There's no reason for him to come after me," she said almost smugly.

"Hell there isn't. He's probably told his men to watch for anyone new in town. You asking questions will surely get his attention," Fargo returned.

"I'll be careful how and what I ask. I've taken a room at the hotel," Brenda said.

"How are you going to explain yourself here?" he pushed.

"I've already done that at the hotel. I've come to meet my family. They're arriving by wagon," she said.

"Dammit, get back to the cabin. I've enough to do just to watch out for myself. I can't watch out for you, too," Fargo said.

"I'm staying right here," she said defiantly, her pale eyes frigid. She'd not be changing her mind until something happened to scare some sense into her. If it wasn't too late by then, Fargo added. But he couldn't just drag her off through town, though he wished he could do as much.

"Just keep your eyes and ears open. Nothing else, understand?" he said. "Where's Hazel?"

"At the cabin. She can't come into town. They'll recognize her. She's useless," Brenda said.

"Pull your claws in and be careful, dammit. I'll check back on you tomorrow," he said and climbed onto the pinto. He didn't want to be seen talking to her, for her own good, and he spurred the horse into a trot as he rode through town in the dusk. Keeping one eye on things to his rear, he circled out of town, slipping into the woods, certain he hadn't been followed. Darkness fell as he made his way back to the cabin. Hazel was there at the door, her rifle in one hand. He unsaddled the Ovaro and put the horse on a long tether so he could have plenty of room to graze. Hazel's eyes locked on him as he strode into the cabin. "No need to tell me. I met her in town," he said crossly.

"I told her you'd be angry," Hazel said.

"She's stubborn," Fargo said.

"She's not just stubborn. She only thinks about what

she wants. That's why she didn't give a damn about the settlers," Hazel said.

"She's as concerned about Harley and the others as you are. I told you that," Fargo reiterated.

"I'll say it again. The same, but different," Hazel returned.

"Meaning what, exactly?" Fargo frowned.

"I don't know exactly but I know I'm right," Hazel snapped. He wanted to ignore Hazel's reply as just cattiness but he couldn't. Right or wrong, Hazel wasn't the catty type. She was being honest about her feelings, uninformed or not.

"You won't be needing your bedroll tonight," Hazel said, in a much different tone now.

"You mean I can use the other cot," he said.

"You won't be needing that, either," she said and followed him to the narrow cot. She was already shedding her clothes, and in moments stood beautifully naked before him, a taunting little smile on her lips. "Still approve? You've seen it before," she said.

"I never said so," he answered.

"You didn't have to. It was in your eyes," Hazel said and waited motionless while he pulled off his own clothes, stepping to him when he finished. Her breasts brushed against his chest, then flattened as she pressed harder against him. He felt her dark pink nipples press into him, a wonderfully soft and provocative sensation. His hands slid down the sides of her body, finding curves more quietly rounded than he remembered, and pressed her down onto the cot. Her figure held together in a neat package. His hands moved slowly down her body, across her modest breasts, and she trembled when he paused at each little tip. He dropped his hands downward, feeling the firmness of her lower body, of hips gently rounded, the tiny convexity of her belly, and the small dense triangle of hair below.

Slowly, he brought his hands up along her body again and she gave a shudder of pleasure, her mouth opening to find his. Her tongue darted forward, sought his, probed, silently pleading, and he answered. She clung, mouth to mouth, lips to lips, tongue to tongue, and her body writhed as it responded to his touch. He brought his lips down to her neck and slid his mouth down the side of her throat, tracing a path along her collarbone. He heard her soft gasping sighs grow stronger. He found one breast, and drew on it, letting his lips gently ply on the little dark pink nubs, and surround the raised circle around it, caressing the edges with his tongue.

He drew the soft sweet mound into his mouth and Hazel's body twisted as she gasped. He continued to caress her breast, sucking it deeper into his mouth, holding it there as his tongue passed back and forth over her nipples.

"Oh, good, good . . . oh, yes, yes," Hazel breathed and shuddered with pleasure. Her fingers dug into his shoulders as he shifted his lips downward, across the flatness of her abdomen, slowly followed by his hand traveling across her little belly, massaging her gently. Hazel groaned, a smile in the sound. His hand moved down further and her legs lifted and straightened, staying tight against each other. His hand paused at the edge of her little V and Hazel's voice rose, crying out in anticipation. He touched further, pressing down on the rise of her pubic mound. She half screamed as his fingers became lost in the jungle of soft fibrous tendrils.

He continued the soft pressure on her mound and she cried out little yelps of delight. When his exploring brought him down to the sudden moistness of her, the touch sent his own excitement spiraling, their senses responding to each other, reasserting itself by touch, feel, and taste. "Please, please," Hazel murmured and her torso pushed upward, her wetness spilling over in the eternal welcome. When he touched the sweet lips of her dark and secret places Hazel's scream burst forth, a cry of plight and demand. He felt her hands pulling at him and he moved his body on top of hers and his pulsating warmth touched her. Hazel cried out again, a sharp, insistent cry and her hips rocked from side to side, upward, back down, upward again as her portal sought fulfillment. "Yes, my God, yes, yes, yes," she shouted almost savagely. He moved with her, brought her the answer she wanted, touched tenderness to tenderness, softness to softness, stoking throbbing warmth to a quivering fire.

"Oh, jeez, oh, my God, my God, yes, oh, yes!" Hazel screamed, her words becoming cries, wild, eager, rapturous sounds. She thrust upward for him, pressed herself tightly to him, wanting to absorb every part of his pulsating gift. She gasped, moaned, screamed, gave of herself with every pushing, thrusting motion. Her neat, contained figure was directed with inner pleasure, her modest breasts heaving and quivering, echoing their passion. The sounds of rapture rising from her suddenly seemed to break off and her silence was startling. Fargo peered at her, and saw her eyes were tightly shut and then he felt her quickening contractions. Her arms tightened against him and he felt her thrusting hard into him, lifting, rubbing her soft portal against him. "Now, now, now, oh, God, now!" Hazel gasped out and the silence was broken, her body trembling violently.

Yet there was no flinging of legs or arms, no frantic convulsions of passion, just an intense, directed, total absorption of the senses. She clung to him, every part of her clamped against him as a limpet clings to a rock, her breasts lifted to push into his face as shuddering pleasure coursed through her. But the transience of ecstasy was not to be denied and, with a shuddered cry of despair, he felt Hazel's body seem to deflate, then fall back on the bed. He stayed with her as her thighs held him tight. "Yes, oh, yes, please," she murmured, something close to a sob in her voice.

He held her, slowly stroking her body as the little contractions inside her still conveyed delicious moments of sensual pleasure. Hazel murmured with her eyes half closed, satisfaction wreathing her face. Finally, she lay still with him, arms at her sides, her body neatly folded against him. Somehow, she could change from eager wanting to a quiet sweetness, from being passionate to being proper, all with her naked loveliness unaffected. Her hand rose, stroked his chest. "I was afraid this would never be mine again," she murmured. "But you have ended that fear. You have been, quote, *a wilderness of sweets.*"

"Quoting who?"

"Milton, *Paradise Lost,* Book Four." Hazel smiled. "An actor lives by quotes."

"Let's hope tonight is not a last time for either of us," Fargo said.

"You think it might be?" she asked, alarmed at once.

"We're dealing with a man who made a whole town disappear. What's a few more victims?" Fargo said.

She shuddered. "I wish I could help more in some way."

"Maybe I'll think of one," he said. "Meanwhile, you keep trying to remember anything Harley said to you about his plans or that prospector." She nodded, snuggled and was asleep against him in minutes.

He lay with her, letting himself sleep, and the night rolled on. He didn't know how long he'd slept when he awoke, his ears instantly picking up the sound of the Ovaro as the horse snorted. He sat up and heard the horse snort again. Something had disturbed him. Hazel stayed fast asleep as Fargo rose to listen, hearing only the sound of the Ovaro's hooves as the horse moved on its long tether. A grim smile edged Fargo's lips and, in a crouch, he crept into the other room and lay down on the cot, pulling the sheet carelessly over him. Closing his eyes, his ears picked up the sound of a second horse, then soft footsteps.

He lay still, feigning sleep, hearing the footsteps pause in the cabin doorway, then turn and slip away. He sat up and crept to the window and watched Brenda pull herself onto her horse, then carefully walk the animal into the trees. He lay back on the cot, a tiny laugh in his throat, and returned to sleep. When dawn came, he washed and dressed and saw Hazel still asleep, curled into a ball. She awoke when he'd finished dressing, sitting up and looking improperly lovely. "I didn't hear you get up," she murmured, rubbing sleep from her eyes.

He stepped to her and she leaned against him at once. "I'm going now. You stay here and be safe," he said.

"I remembered something. It must have come to me as I slept," she said. "Harley was given something by the old prospector, something that he was very excited about."

"He never said what?" Fargo questioned and she shook her head. "What do prospectors have to give?" Fargo prompted.

She thought for a moment. "The location of a mine? Pinpointing a rich vein?"

"Bull's-eye," Fargo said. "Now, you stay here and keep thinking."

"I want to do more," she said.

"At the right time and place," he said.

"When will that be?"

"When I find it," he said and left her. He saddled the Ovaro, gave the horse a quick brushing, and set out through the cottonwoods. He scanned the land on all sides of him as he neared town. Main Street was busy with traffic, and so Fargo drew behind a building to watch undetected. Two men walked along one side of the street, two others on the other side. A third pair on horseback followed a dozen yards behind them. Fargo allowed himself a small smile. Eakins had his men out searching for him. Backing the pinto, he turned and rode along the rear of the buildings until he reached the hotel. He tied the horse to a stanchion and crept along the narrow space between the hotel and the house beside it. He reached Main Street and saw that Eakins's searchers had moved on.

He slipped into the hotel just as Brenda came into the lobby. "You're here. Good. I want to talk," she said.

"Not here," he said.

"Then in my room," she said and he followed her into a ground floor room furnished in typical hotel style with a bed, a battered dresser, and a worn stuffed chair. Tiny lights danced in their pale blue depths of her eyes as she regarded him, her hand coming to rest against his chest. "Been thinking about you, about everything," she said.

He let one eyebrow lift. "Why?" he asked.

"I was wrong about you, and things I said," Brenda murmured, her fingers toying with his shirt.

"How?" he asked.

"Your concern for the settlers. I should have been more understanding," she said.

"Confession is good for the soul," Fargo said mildly as his thoughts went to her stealthy visit in the middle of the night. "How about my concern for Hazel?"

"I misjudged that, too," she said.

"Why the turnabout?" he questioned, keeping his voice mildly curious.

Her smile held a note of smugness. "It just came to me during the night. I realized I shouldn't be so cynical," Brenda said.

"Nights can change a person's thinking," he said blandly.

She leaned forward and brushed his lips with a light touch that held a fleeting moment of electricity. "For understanding," she murmured before he could ask. "What are you going to do now? I want to help."

"I still think Eakins is holding Harley and the rest of the troupe. He has to feed them to keep them alive. Eleven people will take a fair amount of food every day. I'm going to keep a watch at his place. I'll follow his boys when they move the food. That'll lead us to where he's holding everyone," Fargo said.

"What can I do?" Brenda asked.

"He might be picking up tinned food at the general

store. I can't be in two places at once. I want you watching the store. If you see men leave with big sacks, maybe boxes, you watch which way they go out of town."

"How do I tell you?" she asked.

"Come back to the hotel. I'll check in with you," he said and she nodded, brushing his lips again as he started to leave. Outside, he retraced his path along the rear of the town, making his way into the trees and back to a place where he could watch the Eakins spread. He settled down and as the hours rolled on, he saw Sam Eakins three times when he stepped outside to greet another dozen gunhands as they arrived. Fargo's brow furrowed as the question asked itself. Why did Eakins need so many gunhands? Was he afraid of something? Or was he planning something? Tabling pointless speculation, Fargo concentrated on watching the house, the barn, and the corrals. But as the hours rolled on, he saw nothing that in any way resembled food being moved, so he decided to patrol the roads that stretched beyond the Eakins spread.

Perhaps the man was moving food from another source, a shed somewhere, Fargo reasoned, and he traveled the roads and surveyed them from high ground. All he saw were lone riders and one grizzled figure driving two burros laden with sacks, shovels, and axes sticking from their tops. When the day began to draw to a close, Fargo made his way back to town, again carefully moving along the rear of the buildings until he reached the hotel. Brenda was in her room waiting. "See anything?" Fargo asked.

"Just ordinary folks buying ordinary things, and one prospector with two burros," she said.

"Tools sticking out of his sacks?" Fargo asked and she nodded. "I saw him on the road. We'll give it another go tomorrow and if nothing happens, we'll try watching at night."

Brenda's face tightened. "I don't like all this watching and waiting while time's going by," Brenda said. "Don't like it at all."

"I don't like it either, but we can't just go and attack Eakins. I'd say we were a little outnumbered," Fargo remarked.

"I still don't like it," Brenda muttered.

"Got any better ideas?" he asked.

"Not yet," she answered darkly.

"Same thing tomorrow, then. I'll check in here later," he said.

She turned to him. "You don't have to go all the way back to the cabin."

"You offering?" he slid at her.

Her arms slid around his neck, her lips pressed against his, and again he felt the electricity of her touch. "No, not yet," she murmured and stepped back. "Take a room here."

"I'm going back to the cabin. Hazel remembered something. The old prospector told Harley something he got very excited about. I want to see if Hazel's remembered anything more," Fargo said.

Brenda shrugged and stepped back. "Look for you tomorrow," she said, closing the door after him. Fargo returned to the Ovaro and rode into the new night. Would she be paying another stealthy midnight visit to the cabin? he wondered. She was playing her own game with him, he realized. Was it just instinctive female suspiciousness or her need to be in charge?

Or was it hard for her to trust? Those pale blue eyes were a curtain, impossible to see behind. Brenda was an intriguing combination, a promise wrapped in a puzzle.

5

The cabin was dark when he rode up and he felt an instant of fear shoot through him. But a candle flickered to life as he dismounted and Hazel came to the door. "Good God, I've waited for you," she said. "I've been going crazy waiting, jumping out of my skin at every little noise outside."

"You managed hiding in that cave," he said.

"It was quiet there and there were places I could run to," she said as she clung to him. "You find out anything?"

"No. Did you remember anything more?" he questioned.

"One thing. Harley told us he was afraid he'd talked too much one night at the Pleasure Palace."

"That means a lot of people might have been after him," Fargo said. "But why go after the rest of the actors."

"Harley always spoke of us as one, involved in everything together, sharing in everything, a troupe in every sense," Hazel said. "Anyone after Harley would include us."

"I'm staying after Eakins. He's the one with the money and the men," Fargo said.

"You must be hungry and tired," Hazel said and

turned to the wood stove. She had heated some chicken legs and he ate them ravenously. "What happens tomorrow?" she asked when the meal was finished.

"More of the same. It's still our best chance to find where he's got Harley," Fargo said.

"It's taking too long," she said.

"You sound like Brenda," he said.

"Except that I'm really afraid for Harley and everyone else," Hazel returned.

"Why don't you think she is?" Fargo frowned.

"Because I think she cares mostly about herself."

"That's pretty harsh. You could be misjudging her."

"Maybe, but it's what I feel," she said. She was sure stubborn, he saw. But the wanting, eager part of her surfaced quickly when he came to the cot. Once again, they combined sweetness and passion and her own brand of ecstasy, and when the final moments of pleasure ended she quickly slept in his arms.

He stayed with her, but as the night wore on he woke and slid from the cot, and went into the other room and lay down. He still didn't expect another visit from Brenda but he was unwilling to take the chance. Even his feral hearing was not infallible and Brenda was a promise he didn't want to see pulled away before it had a chance of delivery. Pulling sleep around himself, he stayed in the room until dawn woke him, and he was dressed when Hazel sat up and called out for him.

"Right here," he replied as he stepped into the other room. She reached her arms out and he came to her, holding her lovely, smooth skin against him. "You're making it tough for me to leave," he murmured.

"That's the idea. I don't want to sit around here all day again," she muttered.

"One more day," he told her. "Maybe I'll get back earlier. If I don't, stay here. I may be chasing down something." She nodded unhappily and he left her to hurry outside, and was riding into the cottonwoods as the sun filled the forest. Had Brenda paid a midnight visit without his hearing her? he wondered as he rode. A line of horsemen pushing through the trees in front of him broke off his thoughts and he pulled the pinto to a halt in a thick cluster of foliage. He counted twelve Shoshoni as they slowly made their way downhill toward the low ground. They were a hunting party, with no war paint on their ponies, though they'd eagerly descend on any vulnerable target, he knew. After they'd gone their way he moved on and rode downward along the shore of the Yellow River until, skirting the town, he drew up in the trees beside Eakins's place. The scene was much the same, Fargo saw at once, but he watched with a spurt of new interest as Sam Eakins and two of his men rode off toward town.

Fargo fought down the urge to follow them, deciding to depend on Brenda's surveillance at the general store. They reappeared a little over an hour later carrying a half-dozen small bank sacks. Fargo watched as Eakins distributed what was plainly the payroll to all the hands who lined up. When he finished, he returned to the house, and nothing else occurred. Once again, Fargo decided to patrol the roads and this time he saw two family-filled Conestogas along with an assortment of lone riders. The grizzled prospector, with his two burros laden with sacks of tools, came into sight again and Fargo watched him slowly struggle up into the hills. It became a fruitless repeat of the day before and as the day drew toward an end Fargo decided on a night watch. When he reached the hotel, he found Brenda waiting for him in her room, her face set tightly.

"No more watching. It's not working," she said.

"We haven't tried by night. He's got to be getting food to them somehow," Fargo said.

"You could watch for another week before you spot them," Brenda said. "I'm not waiting that long. I've decided on my own way to get to Eakins."

Fargo felt his brows lift in surprise. "You want to let me in on it?" he said.

"No," she said flatly and he felt another stab of surprise.

"I thought we were working together," he said.

"Correction. You're working for me," Brenda said haughtily.

Fargo's eyes narrowed at her. "You do change moods," he commented.

"I don't remember your asking me if you could go save those settlers," she tossed back.

"One for you," he conceded. "But I still want to know what you're planning."

"Later," she said.

"Later could be too late," Fargo said.

"It won't be," she said.

"I don't like it," he answered.

Her arms came up, encircled his neck, her mood changed now. "I'll tell you everything later. Promise," she said.

"Another promise?"

Her mouth came to his, her lips pressing hard, growing wet. "My lips and my word on it," she murmured when she stepped back.

"Still don't like it," he said stubbornly.

"You will. You'll like everything," Brenda said. He tried to see something behind her eyes to let him either believe or doubt, be understanding or suspicious. But there was only the pale azure mask of her blank stare.

"When?" he asked.

"Give me a couple of hours," Brenda said. "Then we'll talk again." Fargo let a snort escape his lips as he turned and strode from the room. He returned to the Ovaro but he didn't ride away just yet. He realized he was unable to put aside the mixture of feelings he had; resentment, surprise, frustration, distrust. They all added up to something he disliked yet he couldn't do otherwise. Brenda had hired him, and brought him here, and now she was shutting him out, going her own way. Was she that impatient? That disappointed in him? It didn't fit. Whatever they'd learned, he had uncovered. He heard Hazel's words echoing inside him: *she cares mostly about herself.*

He moved the horse through the narrow passageway until he could see the door of the hotel and it was but a few moments before Brenda emerged, climbing onto her horse at the hitching post and riding down Main Street. He followed, staying far back, his frown deepening as he saw her leave town, headed on toward the Eakins place. When she neared the spread, Fargo cut into the hills. He stayed at the edge of the trees and when he reached the Eakins house, he halted, dropped from the saddle, and tethered the pinto to a low branch. He hurried forward on foot to the rear of the big house, and started to bend into a crouch when he saw Brenda draw up to the front of the house. Two guards barred her way as she dismounted and started toward the front door.

Fargo was already at the rear of the house, darting out of sight behind the walls and moving to the rear door. He found it locked, then tried a window and had more success as it lifted quietly. He crawled through the opened window, dropped into a dark hallway inside, seeing lamps lighting the front of the house. He crept forward along the hallway, noting that it opened onto a back entrance to the big living room. Two lamps lighted the room. The voices came to him, Sam Eakins's, first, then Brenda's. Fargo dropped to one knee behind a sideboard, where he could see both Brenda and Eakins as they sat down opposite each other. Eakins's eyes devoured Brenda and her pale yellow blouse that mirrored the color of her corn silk hair, lying lightly on her breasts. Brenda's eyes had an edge of confident hardness in them he had never seen before.

"I didn't expect anyone tonight," Eakins said. "Now, what brings me such a lovely visitor?"

"Not small talk. And not to waste your time or mine," Brenda said.

"Very good. Brenda, you said your name was, right?" Eakins smiled with an oily politeness as his eyes continued to roam over Brenda's assets.

"I'm here to find my cousin, Harley Connagher," she said.

"That's nice, but why come to me, my dear?" Eakins said.

Brenda's smile was chiding, frosted with ice. "You have Cousin Harley. The rest of his troupe, too, but Harley's the only one I care about," she said.

Sam Eakins tried to hide the surprise that flooded

his face and failed. "I don't know what you're—" he began as Brenda cut him off.

"Please, no bullshit," she said impatiently, her voice like iron. "You made the whole goddamn town disappear, and Harley along with it."

Sam Eakins was obviously flustered. Fargo saw his face reddening as he tried to recover. "A town disappear? You must have been talking to that lunatic named Fargo. He gave me the same story about the town."

"Yes, I've been talking to him. I hired him and I know what he found so stop the games. I'm here with a proposition that will save us both a lot of time. Are you interested or aren't you?" Brenda pressed. Fargo found himself in awe of her boldness. Eakins smiled nervously but his eyes had narrowed at her.

"Let's say you've made me curious enough to play along with you," he offered. "What kind of proposition are you talking about?"

"I know about Harley and the old prospector," Brenda said. "My proposition will make us both happy. You haven't gotten anything out of Harley, and you won't. He's principled and stubborn. He believes in honor and integrity. He's also an actor and you've given him a role to play. And he'll play it all the way—it's in his blood. He'll be Shakespeare's Richard the Second. 'Mine honor is my life, both grow in one; take honor from me and my life is gone.' He'll feel it and be it and live it. You'll never get what you want from Harley."

"But you can," Eakins said.

"He'll listen to me. I can get him to talk," she said.

"About what?" Eakins smiled.

"You know. The old prospector told him something.

86

You're convinced it means gold. I expect it does too, and I'll find out for sure."

"What makes you so sure of that?"

"Because he sent for me." Brenda laughed and enjoyed the surprise in Eakins's face. "You didn't know about that, of course. Harley's always valued my judgment and he trusts me implicitly."

"What's your price?" Eakins stabbed back.

"Half of everything, whatever it comes out to be," she said firmly.

"If I've done all the things you say, I can go the rest of the way alone. Why should I cut you in for half?" Eakins questioned.

"Because without me you'll get nothing, and half is better than nothing," Brenda said. "Now you tell *me* something. Why so many gunhands? What are you expecting?"

"Cousin Harley was drunk one night at the Pleasure Palace. He said his prospector friend told him a secret that concerned some open public land. That means every Tom, Dick, and Harry could come rushing in. I'm going to make sure that doesn't happen," Eakins said.

"Which means plenty of gunhands," Brenda said. "It fits why Grange disappeared. If rumors got out, nobody could come digging around a town that doesn't exist."

Eakins smiled. "I think we'd make very good partners, Brenda," he said. "Except one thing bothers me. How do I know you won't be off with Cousin Harley if I produce him?"

"Run? With all the men you have to chase us down?" Brenda said mockingly.

"What happens to Cousin Harley if we split fifty-

fifty? You telling me you're just going to toss him aside?" Eakins questioned, the question an echo of the one that rose in Fargo's mind.

"Harley owes me from years back and he won't have to know until it's too late," Brenda said. Fargo had trouble believing his ears.

"What about the others? They're all so damn loyal to him, and to each other," Eakins queried.

"When Harley goes along with me, they'll go along with him," Brenda said.

"What if they don't? I don't like surprises," Eakins insisted.

"I don't really care about the others. You take care of it," Brenda said, and Fargo felt astonishment curling through him.

"You've got it all figured. You're some package, honey," he said.

"Save the compliments till it's done. Do your part. Give me Harley. I'll do the rest," she said.

There was a new admiration in the way Eakins looked at Brenda. Fargo felt a different kind of admiration for Brenda, one made of astonishment and disillusion, perhaps even distrust as he found himself wondering what Brenda was all about. Stupid näiveté or icy selfishness? A kind of reckless boldness or ruthless ambition? She had gone from a puzzle to a paradox. Who was she? *What* was she? The questions tore at him, his eyes locked on her pale loveliness as she rose.

"I'm finished talking," she said to Eakins.

He continued to elect to play carefully. "If I could do the things you think I can, where would I bring Harley?" Eakins asked.

"My hotel room. I'll stay there. I want time alone

with Harley," she answered. "Tomorrow night," she added firmly.

"What about this Fargo? He can be trouble. He's not a man you're going to wrap around your finger. Believe me," Eakins said.

Brenda gave him a smile as dazzling as it was unexpected. "I'm good at wrapping. Believe me," she murmured as Eakins started to show her to the door. Fargo was already backing down the dark hall to the rear window. He crawled back through it, touching the ground on the balls of his feet as the two guards came around the corner of the house, both carrying rifles. Obviously making a routine patrol, they didn't hurry and Fargo had the chance to duck behind a rhododendron bush at the corner of the house. The two guards had almost passed the spot when one stopped.

"Benny, look at this window. It's open," one said and Fargo cursed inwardly.

"Maybe Eakins left it open," the other said.

"Shit, you know how he is on closing windows. He's always hollering about it," the first man said and stepped to the window, leaning his rifle against the wall and pushing his head inside. "I don't like it," he muttered.

Fargo knew he needed one thing above all else—silence. One shot, one shout, and they'd be coming from all sides. Every muscle taut, he sprang forward as if catapulted, his hands closing around the rifle. He brought it up in a short, vicious uppercut, the barrel catching the man on the point of the jaw just as he started to pull away from the window. He collapsed instantly but the second guard had turned. Fargo sent the rifle hurtling through the air as if it were a spear.

The point of the barrel slammed into the man's throat and the man dropped his rifle, clutching at his neck with both hands as he sank to the ground and lay still. Fargo raced away through the darkness to the Ovaro and walked the horse quietly through the trees.

They'd find the two guards in time and Eakins would suspect the truth without being certain. It would make him wonder about Brenda's visit. Fargo smiled as he made his way through the cottonwoods, finally reaching the shore of the Yellow River back to town. He reached the hotel, still churning inside, but he'd reached a decision. He'd not let the turmoil inside him affect caution. He had to stab at her, to shake her up, to see what he could pull from her yet not reveal what he himself knew. When she opened the door, he stormed into the room. "Why, goddammit, *why*? What the hell are you thinking?" he flung at her.

She frowned in surprise. "How did you know?" she asked.

"I followed you, saw you go to the Eakins place," Fargo said, leaving out anything more. "What did you think you could do?"

"Get Harley back," Brenda said.

"How?" he pushed at her.

"With reason, logic, fact," Brenda said almost haughtily.

"I'm listening," he snapped and she proceeded to tell him about her visit. She spoke firmly, recounting almost everything about her meeting with Eakins. But the parts she didn't mention turned his stomach sour. When she finished, she had given him a story accurate enough to be entirely plausible. He might well have believed it, he realized, had he not listened to the real thing. But he had to prod her further. "You're telling me you sweet-talked a man like Eakins into going along with you?" he said.

"I didn't sweet-talk him. I convinced him he was wasting his time," Brenda said. "I told him I was the only one who could find out what he wanted to know."

"I still can't buy it," Fargo muttered.

"I can be very convincing. You'll see when he brings Harley to me," she said.

He prodded her again and knew inside he was desperately hoping she'd tell him the things she had left out and wipe away the bitter taste in his mouth. "What happens after you tell Eakins what he wants to find out?" Fargo pressed.

"I'll convince him he has to make some sort of deal with Harley," she said and Fargo cursed silently as he thought about the dastardly deal she had struck with Sam Eakins.

"Why didn't you tell me what you were planning to do?" he pushed at her.

"Would you have agreed?" she returned sharply. "No, you'd have argued and argued. You might even have tried to stop me. I couldn't have that."

He glared at her even as he knew that in this case she was completely right. "I always try to stop fools from committing suicide," he said, letting her feel he had accepted her story. "Here's a man who's made a town disappear, killed at least half the people there, and took the others prisoner. You know what kind of a deal he'll make with you after you tell him what he wants to know from Harley? One that'll make you dead, along with your cousin."

Brenda stared back and Fargo knew a sudden realization had stabbed at her behind her opaque eyes.

He'd spelled out something that would apply equally to the deal she had worked out with Eakins, an ominous possibility she hadn't considered. "I hadn't thought about that," she admitted and he knew there was no guile in her voice. She stared soberly into space for another minute, then her arms came around him. "I'll be counting on you to stop that from happening," Brenda murmured.

"I'm kind of short on miracles," Fargo said.

"I'm not," she said. Her lips pressed to his, her body clung tight, and her fingers began to open the blouse. It fell away from her, sliding to the floor, letting Fargo see her broad shoulders and a wide rib cage supporting beautifully formed breasts that curved in lovely lines right down to very full, rounded cups. He stared at skin so delicately white it almost matched the pale blue of her eyes. Small nipples of the palest pink on circles of matching paleness peeked out at him. She pushed on her skirt and it slid from her hips and he took in a hard flat stomach, thin but still curving thighs, and a delicately soft bush that almost glistened. She led him to the bed, her breasts swaying, inviting.

Fargo grimaced inside himself, feeling as though he were divided, part of him ready to respond to her beauty, and another part of him wondering what he was getting himself into. Would he be in bed with a foolish young woman of total selfishness? Or would he be making love to beauty that was devious, dangerous, and perhaps even evil? The questions circled through him and one answer pushed itself forward. He could only find out by going along with her. He could only know by seeing it to the end. A wry laugh formed inside him. Was he being honest or just giving himself excuses? Reasoning with his head or his loins?

As his eyes stayed on her he decided it was a question he didn't need to answer immediately. There was time. His mouth engulfed one pale-skinned nipple and Brenda moaned at once. He suckled gently, his tongue dancing across the small pale pink tip and her moans grew louder, still louder, and he felt her body churn in rapture. "Oh, please, please," Brenda gasped and arched her breast upward, pushing it deeper into his mouth. "So nice, so good," she murmured. Her delicate paleness seemed to evaporate as suddenly she was twisting, pushing herself hard against him. In her wanting, in her desire, there was nothing pale. Her hands clasped his back, her nails dug in hard.

She came to him with a fervor that swept aside any thoughts of sweet slowness, her body slithering up and down against him. She pressed first one part of her body then another into his face; her mouth, breasts, abdomen, belly, her gossamer triangle, raising her legs to press the wetness of her against him, then sliding downward only to repeat her movements again. "Oh, God, oh, God, yes, oh, God yes," Brenda gasped out and he felt her skin had become moist and warm. He held her tight for a moment, stilling her fervent movements, and then felt her hands reaching for him, clasping around his own pulsating warmth. "Give me, give me," Brenda gasped, her back lifting as her hands began stroking, caressing, pulling, rubbing, her lips moving to him, touching, tasting. Her little cries grew stronger, each one its own little moan of pure pleasure.

Her sudden eruption of desire continued, almost as if the inner person was trying to make up for the contained exterior she presented. He peered at her eyes and saw a new, deep blue flame in their opaqueness, like fire behind glass. Her legs lifted again and she rubbed her pubic mound against his groin, lowering herself to grind her quivering wetness against him, pleading far more powerfully than any words could. It was a command impossible to disobey. He brought his own throbbing iron to her, and slowly slid into her enveloping warmth. Brenda screamed at his touch, a sound of pure, primitive pleasure. Again and again she cried out as he moved inside her, the full cups of her breasts swaying from side to side as her body turned and twisted. With each motion, she seemed to be trying to make flesh do more than it could, forcing her senses to find more and more pleasure.

She seemed impossible to satisfy as her body demanded more and more, her cries escalating to hymns to ecstasy. He thought he detected a note of desperation edging into her voice as that total moment of absolute satisfaction continued to elude her. But suddenly he felt the trembling begin to sweep through her body. Her thighs rose up to clasp him and her trembling grew more violent. "Oh, God, oh, oh, oh!" Brenda cried out, her voice rising, and the scream burst from her as her entire body violently shook as cry after cry burst from her. Her full-cupped breasts slapped into his chest as she shuddered, her thighs squeezing hard around him. Fargo could hold back no longer, gushing like a geyser as he pumped furiously into her. When her final scream spiraled into the air it seemed as though the room itself rocked. She hung as if suspended, her mouth open, as though she could gasp in pleasure forever until suddenly, she fell against him, little shudders now coursing through her. "God," she whispered. "Oh, God." She lay still with him, barely breathing until finally he heard her take in slow, long breaths.

She stirred, then sat up looking serenely lovely, a pleased little smile toying with her lips. "Enjoy it?" she remarked.

"Quite a ride," he said.

"Glad you didn't bother chasing after anyone else?" she said smugly.

"Absolutely," he answered.

She nuzzled against him. "I'm yours, whenever and wherever. Just help me with Eakins. I'm real bothered by what you said."

"You should be. Making deals with the devil never works out," Fargo said, keeping his tone casual. "You said he's going to bring Harley to you. What about the others? You never mentioned them."

"I forgot about them," Brenda said and Fargo had to fight down the anger that threatened to spill over, her cold unfeeling words with Eakins rotting inside of him. Brenda was a good actress herself, he decided and wondered if her passion had been acting. But he discarded the thought. She wasn't that good an actress. That part of her, at least, had been very real.

"I'm going to the cabin," he said and she frowned.

"Why? There's no reason," Brenda said.

"Hazel expected me long ago. I don't want her to panic and run off and get into more trouble," he said, the answer not untrue. Brenda shrugged dismissively. "You want me here when he brings Harley?" Fargo asked.

She thought for a moment. "No. Let Harley and

me be alone. You wait outside. I'll come down and get you," she said.

"Your show," Fargo said and pulled on his clothes. Brenda stayed beautifully naked, plainly enjoying the effect and the message. He admitted it took an effort for him to leave but when he rode from town his thoughts returned to Brenda in another way. He had very much enjoyed making love to her but it had answered no questions. She'd let nothing slip, revealing only her ardent passion. Regardless of how real it was, she still used it to further her needs, and bitterness flooded through him again. Her lie about the troupe stabbed at him, her icy words with Eakins reverberating in his thoughts. Which Brenda was the real one? he wondered. The one trying to outwit Sam Eakins or the one out to betray everyone for her own ends. He rode on, turning the question over in his mind with increasing bitterness.

Hazel awoke when he reached the cabin, running to him with a sheet wrapped around herself. "I was so worried," she said, clinging to him.

"I told you I could be late," he said as he hugged Hazel's neat, contained figure. Everything about her was so different from Brenda.

"You have to let me help," Hazel said.

"Not yet. Brenda made contact with Sam Eakins. She thinks she can make a deal with him," Fargo told her.

"Will that bring back the people he killed?" Hazel snapped.

Fargo cursed inwardly, her question a reminder that Eakins hadn't even mentioned that. Neither had Brenda. He felt weariness sweep over him, so he pulled off his clothes and lay back on the cot. Hazel curled up alongside him and he let sleep become a refuge.

When morning came, Hazel made coffee. As she sat across from him, she asked, "What now?"

"I'll see Harley Connagher myself tonight. I'll know more then," Fargo said. After they finished their coffee, Fargo rode from the cabin with plenty of waiting time on his hands. He rode into the high hills and found himself moving toward the high fields of squash and camass, where he'd first met Awenita. He straightened in the saddle, growing more alert at once. He was in the heart of Shoshoni country. Letting the Ovaro choose its way, Fargo wandered along the hills when he saw a spiral of smoke from a road below, partly hidden by the thick tree cover. It was gray-white smoke, he saw with a curse, and urged the pinto downward. It was after he'd crossed over the third ridge that he got a good glimpse of the narrow road. At a curve, a few dozen yards on, he saw the still-smoking, charred remains of a Conestoga.

He sent the pinto into a trot and dropped from the saddle when he reached the wagon, the Colt in his hand. Boxes and trunks from inside the Conestoga had been dumped on the ground and broken open. Walking to the other side of the wagon, he found the corpses of two men and two women, a young girl, and two teenage boys. They had tried to put up a fight from behind the side of the wagon, but all were riddled with arrows. He examined the arrow shafts and saw Shoshoni markings near the feathers.

He grimaced as his words to Brenda bubbled up in his mind. She wasn't the only one to make pacts with the devil. The Shoshoni had suffered a stinging defeat when they attacked Jed Hopper and his group. They'd be prone to extract vengeance at every opportunity. A lone Conestoga of foolish dreamers would be a sitting duck for any war party. He walked away, and had pulled himself onto the Ovaro when he saw the six braves push through the trees. One held clothes taken from the wagon in his arms. Fargo's hand rested on the butt of the Colt but he stayed motionless as the six bucks peered hard at him. They recognized him, their eyes made of stone, but they made no move toward him. Slowly, they turned and rode away.

He waited until they were out of sight before he moved on and realized he felt not unlike a man caught up in something he could not properly define, control, or predict. He'd wandered another half mile when he glimpsed the figures far off in a field of squash and camass root. The figures became squaws as he drew closer, a few young girls, mostly older women. Most wore only hide skirts and as he approached the women glanced up but no one fled. They calmly returned to filling their baskets and he grimaced as he knew the reason for their unperturbed attitude. Shoshoni braves were somewhere in the trees nearby. He started to move on when a voice called out from close by.

"Fargo," it said and he turned in the saddle to see Awenita standing near, her copper-tinted, regally handsome face held high. She, too, wore only a hide skirt, decorated with beadwork that formed a stylized eagle. Her long, jet black hair hung in two braids, one lying atop each breast. "Have you come for what is yours to demand?"

"No. Just happened to be this way," he told her.

Her deep, dark eyes held his and he thought he caught a fleeting moment of disappointment touch her smooth, handsome face. "I have waited," the Indian girl said.

"It will be." He nodded, aware that it would be seen as a dishonor for him not to collect on the pact of honor.

"When?" she asked simply.

"Soon," he said, the answer the only one to satisfy her.

"I have wondered if you were alive," Awenita said.

"Very much, as you can see." Fargo smiled.

"I am glad," she said, unsmiling, but he knew the three words meant much more than they said. He'd hurry finishing with Brenda and all the strange and unanswered questions she had brought, he promised himself. He had a simple, straightforward debt to collect that promised only pleasure without complications. The thought was becoming infinitely appealing.

"Soon," he promised again and this time Awenita smiled as she slowly walked from him, moving soundlessly through the grass, her braids letting him see only the sides of her ample breasts. He turned the Ovaro and rode away into the hackberry and found a stream that ran past a clump of wild plums. He dismounted, ate, stretched out, and let the quiet and the warmth of the forest lull him to sleep. The cool of dusk woke him as it slid through the trees. He rose, and rode out of the forest and down from the high hills as night fell. The town was dark when he reached it and this time when he neared the hotel, he concealed himself diagonally across the street from the building where three barrels offered a good hiding spot.

Six men sat their horses in a line along the front of the hotel, with two riderless horses beside them. Sam Eakins had arrived with Harley Connagher. He settled down but he hadn't long to wait before Eakins emerged from the hotel, speaking to the six men and then riding away alone. Fargo watched the six men move away from the front of the hotel and settle down in different places nearby, all staying within the deep shadows. He let a wry smile edge his lips. It wasn't long before Brenda came from the hotel, halting in the doorway to peer into the night. He rose, leading the Ovaro behind him as he crossed the street to her, one hand on the butt of the Colt, his ears straining for a rush of feet or the click of a trigger hammer being pulled back. But he heard nothing, and fastened the Ovaro to the hitching post and followed Brenda into the hotel.

"Eakins left six of his boys watching in case you should decide to run off with Cousin Harley," Fargo told her.

"I suppose that's to be expected," Brenda said.

"There's no honor among thieves," he remarked.

"What's that supposed to mean?" Brenda snapped.

"Just an expression. Maybe it doesn't really fit." He smiled but her glare stayed. "How's Harley?"

"Not bad, considering they burned him with cigars to make him talk," she said. "The others, too, he said."

"This is the kind of man you're making a deal with," Fargo commented.

"I have to. It's saving Harley's life," she said righteously. He didn't answer and her mouth tightened at his silence. Opening the door, she ushered him into the room and Harley Connagher rose to his feet. Fargo saw the man was a little on the portly side, clad in a wrinkled shirt and trousers. Harley Connagher had brown eyes in a soft face that could easily be petulant or stubborn, Fargo saw, full lips, and a hint of jowls that didn't hide a strong chin. He wasn't over thirty, Fargo guessed. "Here he is, the Trailsman you asked me to send for," Brenda introduced.

"Wonderful, wonderful. You're going to be the key to everything, Fargo," Harley Connagher said, his voice taking on a resonance that showed his ability to project on stage.

"Hadn't figured to be that," Fargo said.

"But you will be, you will be," Harley boomed out as if he had taken command of a stage. "I had faith in Brenda and having her bring you. As Brutus says in Julius Ceasar, 'There are no tricks in plain and simple faith.' "

Fargo nodded and hoped that was true for Harley Connagher's sake. Brenda stepped to him and eased him back into the chair.

"First, you have to tell us what this is all about, Harley. I can't help you working in the dark. Neither can Fargo," she said.

"No, of course not. But what of this monster, Eakins? How did you get him to let me go, Brenda?" Harley asked.

"I convinced him you'd never tell him anything," she said.

"You were right. I'd die rather than have anything to do with a man like that," Harley said, his voice ringing out.

Something Brenda had said about Harley flew through Fargo's mind. "You're not just caught up playing a role, are you, Harley?" he asked.

"Absolutely not," Harley thundered and Fargo believed him.

"We don't want you to die, Harley. We don't want

that to happen. It could, of course. Sam Eakins has power and no conscience," Brenda cut in.

"I've seen that," Harley said. "All the more reason not to bow to him. That would be morally indefensible."

"I'm interested in defending your life, Harley," Brenda said soothingly.

"But it's not just my life. It's all the rest of my troupe, too—Bob, Jack, Tom, Keith, Jane, Amy . . . all of them," he said and the concern in his eyes was one of real anguish. Fargo realized he was developing a growing admiration for this soft-faced man with the hard-edged principles. He shifted his gaze to Brenda, curious as to where she was headed and how she was going to get there.

"Maybe none of this is worth your life or anyone's life, Harley," she said. "Maybe I'll see it exactly as you do and maybe I won't. But you have to tell me everything before I can know how to help you with Eakins."

Fargo listened, his thoughts racing. Logical, reasonable words, he had to agree silently and wished he hadn't overheard her meeting with Sam Eakins. Either she had been conning Eakins, or she was conning Harley now. But one thing was certain. She was very cleverly drawing Harley out. Fargo sat back and knew that Harley was going to tell her everything and he felt misgiving course through him. Along with a feeling of utter helplessness.

6

"Start with your prospector, Harley. He had a name, I presume," Brenda suggested.

"Yes. George Dinnard. People called him Crazy George," Harley said.

"Why?"

"Because he was always chasing down diggings, veins, and strikes others had abandoned or in strange places most others rejected," Harley explained. "We met by accident and George was already very sick. He knew he didn't have long to live. I would bring him food and medicine and whatever he needed. That's when he told me he had discovered this vein of gold that would bring millions of dollars."

"Why didn't he try to work it himself?" Brenda asked.

"He was already too ill and too poor. To work it would take a lot of diggers who'd want to be paid. He had neither the money nor the strength left. But he wanted to tell me because I was the only person who had ever befriended him."

"What exactly did he tell you?" Brenda pressed. Fargo heard the excitement that came into her voice.

"George died before he gave me the final, exact location but he had told me enough. He told me he'd discovered the vein that made the Yellow River yellow. You know what that means? A vein big enough and strong enough to wash off enough gold dust to turn a river yellow must be a gigantic strike."

"Why hasn't anyone mined the gold dust and traced the vein before?" Brenda questioned.

"They've tried, hundreds of times. The gold dust in the river is too fine to mine and every exploration has been a failure. Every other prospector decided it's a useless chase, that the gold dust is seeping into the river from some far-off place they'll never find," Harley said.

"How did Crazy George find it?" she said.

"By accident, he told me. A place others explored and gave up on, a vein hidden away. He hadn't told me the exact spot when he died but he left me enough clues. I'm counting on Fargo to decipher them and find the trail to the exact spot," Harley said.

Brenda's eyes went to Fargo. "The riverbank would surely be a public place. Territory officials wouldn't let anyone stake a claim on public land. No wonder Sam Eakins realized he had to prepare to keep everyone else away while he worked the vein."

"He knew he'd never keep it a secret when he started to work the vein, but getting rid of the town would cut down on anyone snooping around and asking questions. You can't chase down rumors in a town that doesn't exist," Fargo said.

Brenda returned to Harley. "How does the rest of the troupe fit in?"

"We all came out here together, with the same dreams. We have a special bond. When I realized what George had given me I told the others we were going to share enough money to make our dreams come true."

"Which were?" Fargo put in.

"To set down a pioneer theater here that would bring pleasure, knowledge, and entertainment for the mind and the heart to all those struggling to make a life here. We'd be the first theater established in the new territory. That alone would give us a place in history. The Pioneer Players, we'd call ourselves," Harley said, growing excited as he spoke. "We'd be following in the footsteps of the ancient Greeks. They built their amphitheaters to bring plays to the ordinary people and the people responded. They came in droves. The medieval craft guilds built theaters, and in Elizabethan times companies of actors like Burbage and Shakespeare built their own theaters. All were for the ordinary people. We'll be following a glorious tradition and the people will come here, too. People have always come to the theater to be told stories, to be taught, entertained, and lifted out of their ordinary lives. It's a basic need."

Harley sat back, his eyes shining, his entire being caught up in the telling of dreams, for a brief moment rising above the reality of Sam Eakins. And perhaps other realities he didn't know about, Fargo muttered to himself.

"This is all very nice, but it doesn't tell me exactly where they fit," Brenda pressed.

"We all signed a contract spelling out how much we'd put into the theater from our share of the gold," Harley said.

"Dammit, did you tell them the clues Crazy George gave you?" Brenda snapped, losing her sympathetic calm for an instant.

"No, I didn't," Harley said. "But Eakins doesn't know that. That's why he's holding them, too. He's afraid I might have." Fargo's glance went to Brenda as thoughts swirled behind her opaque pale blue eyes. Finally, she returned her gaze to Harley.

"This can be worked out. Eakins can actually be important to you," she said and Harley frowned back. "Crazy George knew it would take a lot of time and money and men to find the vein and work it. You don't have either but Eakins has it all—the men, the money, and the time."

"But he's an evil man," Harley muttered. "A monster."

"Look, Harley, don't make your mind up this minute. Sleep on it. Think about it. Look at it as a simple business proposition. You give him the clues and he provides the men and the money to find the vein and work it. I'll convince him to take a small percentage," she said and Fargo marveled at how persuasive and reasonable she could be. Clever.

"I don't need Eakins. Fargo will find the vein for me once I give him the clues," Harley said.

"Then give him the clues now or sleep on it," Brenda countered. "All I want is what's best for you, Harley. If you want to sleep on it, I'll be here in the morning to talk. But I'd rather you gave Fargo the clues, now."

"I think Harley should sleep on it," Fargo interrupted and saw the flash of anger in Brenda's face. Her lips twitched for a moment and she got up, strode to the door, and pulled it open. She motioned for Fargo to follow her outside and slammed the door shut behind him when he did.

"Butt out," she hissed. "What are you trying to do? Why are you interfering?"

"The more he keeps the clues to himself the longer he'll stay alive. I have his best interests at heart," Fargo said.

"So do I," Brenda shot back.

"So you keep saying," Fargo remarked.

"Meaning what?" She glowered.

"Meaning you have *your* best interests at heart," Fargo said. "You know Eakins won't buy that deal you just laid out for Harley. He won't buy any deal, not even the fifty-fifty one you made with him."

Brenda's lips fell open in surprise. "How do you know about that?" she demanded.

"Little birdie told me," Fargo said.

She glared as realization swept through her. "Little birdie my foot! You didn't just follow me to Eakins's place. You got inside. You were listening! That's despicable."

"Not as much as the game you're playing," he said.

"I made the deal with Eakins to get him to let Harley go," she countered. "And it worked."

"I almost believe you," Fargo said sadly.

"I'm doing my best in my own way," Brenda said.

"Me, too." He growled, then brushed past her and went back to the room. "Sleep on the clues till morning. I'll be back then," he said to Harley.

"Whatever you say." Fargo nodded and Brenda was at the door as he left.

"You'll be apologizing tomorrow," Brenda called after him but he kept walking, returning to the Ovaro and riding away. Eakins had kept his men in place, Fargo noted as he left town. He still wanted to believe in Brenda, but she turned and twisted too easily and too glibly. Believing in her was growing more difficult each time. The night was deep and he decided against the long ride back to the cabin. Finding a spot in the trees, he stretched out his bedroll alongside a stream and slept until morning came to wake him. He washed in the stream and returned to the hotel, where Brenda admitted him, wearing a crisply pressed dark red blouse and jeans. He saw Harley already sipping a mug of coffee, his face strained and haggard.

"Been waiting for you, Fargo," he said. "I hardly slept thinking about everything."

"Make your mind up?" Fargo asked.

"I'm not telling Eakins anything. I won't have any dealings with that man. I'd feel soiled," Harley said.

"I told Harley whatever he decided was fine with me," Brenda cut in smoothly. She was going to say more when a heavy pounding on the door stopped her. Brenda answered the door and Sam Eakins and two of his gunhands swept into the room. Fargo quickly let his hand whip to the butt of the Colt at his hip. Eakins fastened a hard glare at Brenda.

"You convince this piss-ant actor to talk?" he threw at her.

"She did not," Harley spoke up firmly.

"I tried. Harley listened. Give me some more time," Brenda said.

"Trying doesn't count, honey," Eakins snapped and fastened his eyes on Harley. "No more playing with you. We'll see how much you care about your precious actor friends. You start talking by tomorrow or I shoot one each day."

Fargo saw horror seize Harley's soft face. "You monster! You rotten, evil excuse for a human being!" he threw at Eakins.

"One each day, one by one," Eakins repeated. "That way they can rehearse their last words. That's my deal. No more talking, no more waiting." He started to stride from the room and paused before Fargo. "I'll get around to you when it's finished," he said threateningly.

"I hope so," Fargo said and Eakins flung a curse back as he left and the door slammed shut. Harley let out a deep groan of despair.

"That's it. There's nothing more to do. It's over," he said. "I'll tell him what he wants to know. I can sacrifice myself, but I can't sacrifice others. I don't have that right. No one does."

"I'll talk to him again. Maybe I can still work out some kind of deal," Brenda put in.

"For who?" Fargo grunted.

"For everyone," she snapped and he made a derisive snort.

"No. Just go to him. Tell him I'll talk. I've no choice any longer," Harley said, anguish in his voice.

"Yes, you do," Fargo replied and drew Harley's eyes to him. "Stall. Make him wait till tomorrow. Give me tonight."

"What are you going to do?" Brenda asked quickly.

"Whatever I can," Fargo said.

"He said tomorrow but what makes you think he'll wait?" Harley questioned. "He's hardly a man to keep his word."

"I don't trust his word. I trust his rotten cunning. He knows the more time you have to agonize the more likely you'll give in."

"Evil understands good. That's always been the problem," Harley said bitterly and stared morosely into space as Fargo walked from the room. Brenda followed him outside and her arms encircled his neck.

"You're misjudging me, Fargo. I can help. I want to," she said. Her lips pressed to his, her mouth opening, inviting. "You've forgotten so soon?" she murmured.

"Hell, no," he said. "That's the trouble."

"You're wrong about me, all wrong," she insisted.

"I've been wrong before. What's one more time?" Fargo said, and pulled her arms from him and started away.

"You're being a bastard," she flung after him. Fargo just nodded as he hurried from the hotel. Outside, he climbed onto the Ovaro, then quickly searched and found the six men watching the hotel from different places. Eakins was taking no chances on Harley trying to bolt in desperation. He wasn't taking chances on Brenda stopping him, either. Fargo smiled. Sam Eakins was not a man who trusted people. It was sad that he was so often right, Fargo muttered to himself as he rode down Main Street. He spotted more of Eakins's men watching the crowds on the street and when he rode from town he carefully checked to be certain he wasn't being followed. Satisfied that he wasn't, he turned into the thick stand of junipers and rode north.

Eakins plainly felt he had all the pieces in hand. All he had to do was keep a careful watch on everything. With one stroke, Eakins had changed everything. His ruthless promise to execute each member of the troupe had given him the winning hand. Harley would not and could not allow that to happen, but there was one way left to deny Eakins his victory—take his hand away from him. Putting the pinto into a trot, Fargo held a steady pace as he made his way back to the cabin. The sun was in the afternoon sky when the cabin came into sight and Hazel ran out to greet him as he dismounted. "You're back. I can't take this waiting and wondering anymore," she said.

"You won't have to. You're on front and center, as Harley would say," Fargo told her and she squealed in delight. "Get your horse and your gear. You're going to town," he said.

Hazel frowned. "To town? Eakins's men will spot me in no time. They're still looking for me. They'll take me," Hazel said.

"Exactly what I'm counting on," Fargo said. "You're going to be the bait for my trap. They'll grab you and they'll take you to wherever they're holding the others. This time I'll find out where, because I'll be following them."

She peered at him. "The lamb staked out for the wolves to find."

"Go to the head of the class. It's the only way to free everyone," Fargo said. "Is it foolproof? No. Things can always go wrong. You can say no if you want. I'll understand."

"I'll get my things," she said and minutes later he was riding beside her.

"I'll disappear when we get near town. You won't see me again till it's over, one way or the other," Fargo told her and she nodded understanding. "When I disappear, you ride in and go to the general store. Act scared, as if you're trying not to be seen. When they take you, fight a little—but only a little. Then go along with them. Just don't go looking around for me."

"I know exactly what to do," she said, without any

nervousness in her voice. "This might be my biggest role ever," she said.

"Maybe," Fargo agreed.

"You better be a damn good understudy." She sniffed and he laughed. The day was growing late when they left the hills and reached the road below. Hazel rode on, her back straight, and suddenly she was alone on the road. She looked around in an instant of surprise and fright, but pulled herself together at once and rode on, her eyes ahead. Fargo had vanished into the hackberry that lined the road, his eyes never leaving her. The town loomed up and the tree cover began to thin. Fargo pushed the pinto onto a rise along the back of the town, riding on ahead of her and dropping from the saddle to make his way on foot. He was behind a tethered one-horse farm wagon when Hazel neared the general store.

His eyes swept the width of Main Street and it was but a few moments more when he saw the six men, three from one side, three from another, move toward the storefront as Hazel halted and slid from her horse. She glanced around furtively and began to scurry toward the store. She was a very good actress. Fargo nodded approvingly. She was almost at the entrance of the store when the men descended on her from both sides, one clapping his hand over her mouth. They pushed her into a narrow alleyway between two buildings while one of them brought their horses.

When they rode from the alleyway, they had Hazel between them. It had taken seconds and nobody on the street had even noticed. Fargo watched them ride off to the other end of town, toward Eakins's place. He retrieved the Ovaro and followed, carefully hanging back. He was waiting in the cottonwoods outside the Eakins spread when they appeared with Hazel and took her inside. Dusk was starting to slide over the land, Fargo noted, when three men left the house with Hazel, loaded her onto her horse, and rode away with her. Fargo allowed himself a moment of satisfaction as he followed at a careful distance. So far it had all gone as he'd hoped it would. They had seized the bait and were on their way to wherever they were holding the others. He followed as they headed north toward the Salmon River Mountains, moving closer as night descended. He guessed another hour had passed when he caught the glow of lamplight through the trees.

Carefully, he moved a dozen yards closer and saw a long, narrow structure given shape by three large kerosene lamps hanging from its walls. He peered at the structure, and recognized it as an old logging camp building, the kind used to bunk thirty or more men on mattresses. Broken awls, an ax handle, and a rusted oil can affirmed his quick evaluation. But bars had been put across the four windows of the long building, he noted. Five men came from behind the house as the three halted with Hazel and pulled her down from her horse. They spoke with the three new arrivals and Hazel was soon pushed into the house. Fargo heard the shouts of greeting from inside.

Fargo's eyes scanned the men, the five who had been there and the three who brought Hazel. There didn't seem to be any others, but the three new arrivals were plainly going to stay. One man made sure that the door of the house was bolted shut before everyone walked back behind the long, narrow structure. Fargo could hear their voices, guessing that there was a small bunkhouse or tents behind the large bunkhouse. He grimaced. Eight guards. Hardly appealing odds. He'd hoped for three or four. In a half crouch, he sprinted across the small open space to one of the four windows in the long bunkhouse. Carefully, he rose up just enough to let himself peer inside. The first thing he saw was the mattresses stacked in one corner, with more laid out on the floor. His eyes went to the figures that were clustered together, at least three embracing Hazel. Five men and five women, Fargo counted, all a few years younger than Harley. But there were no additional guards inside, and Fargo was grateful for that much.

Sliding away from the window, Fargo returned to the trees and took the big Henry from its saddle case. He paused, his mind racing to find a way to get the troupe out. He thought of unbolting the door and trying to sneak everyone out, but soon discarded the idea. They'd never be quiet enough, and the guards were directly behind the house. They'd hear the attempt. Besides, Fargo reminded himself, an escape would take horses. Fargo cursed softly as he ran through other ideas, none of them offering much chance for success. Once the shooting started, Eakins's men would have the advantage. They could take to the trees and bushes around the house and keep everyone pinned down. Eakins was sure to arrive sooner or later with the rest of his force.

If there was to be shooting, Fargo decided, it had to be on his terms, with him holding the first advantage. His eyes swept the roof of the long structure but there was no chimney to let him crawl down. He swore again. He had devised a way to find the troupe, but finding and freeing were very different. As he kept discarding plans, one thing grew all-important. He had to reduce the odds and there was but one way to do it. He had to bring them out where they'd be targets, and only boldness and surprise could do that. He moved forward with the rifle, his mouth a tight, grim line. He'd be taking the ultimate risk but there was no other way.

Halting, he took aim and fired three shots. The three big kerosene lamps hanging on the wall of the house shattered at almost the same instant. They became a cascade of flame that swept the ground and against the wall of the longhouse. In seconds they were devouring grass and twigs on the ground and licking at the wall of the house. The space in front of the house was no longer held by the night; it was now a flaming inferno.

"What the hell . . . ?" he heard one of the men shout, followed by pounding footsteps as they ran from behind the house. They skidded to a halt as they came face-to-face with the growing fire, some of the individual pockets of flame joining together. Fargo saw each of the men clearly outlined by the fire. The rifle's heavy sound drowned out the crackling flames. Three of the men went down as though they'd been pulled by an invisible lasso. A fourth staggered a few paces before collapsing. Two of the others dived to the ground, rolling away, and Fargo swung the rifle toward a seventh figure trying to race around the end of the house.

The man pitched forward and Fargo swore as he saw the flames moving up the wall of the house as if they were so many fast-moving fiery caterpillars. The last three of the guards had hit the ground and had come up firing. Fargo rolled across the grass as bullets flew by just inches from him, propping himself up against a corner of the house. The last three guards had dropped down into bushes and Fargo heard screams from inside the house. He saw the flames eagerly devouring the old wood, smoke already pouring into the sky. He tried moving away from the corner but a hail of bullets slammed into the ground at his feet.

He ducked back but not before he threw another glance at the long house. The flames and the smoke were engulfing the side and the door. He cursed in frustration. Even if he fought the flames and smoke and managed to open the bolt, it would be a death trap for those inside. They'd come running out and Eakins's men would pick them off as they did. He paused another split second and started to race around to the rear of the house. He knew he was risking everything, literally playing with fire. Reloading the rifle as he ran, Fargo dropped low at the other end of the house, peering into the bushes. The three guards were hunkered down but the flames were burning high now. They revealed the three figures as dark shadows, poised in the brush, but clearly outlined. Fargo fired three quick shots just as he knew time was running out, the crackle of the flames now deafening.

Two of the men went down together, the third half rose, fired back, and collapsed. Fargo rose and ran out into the open, where the flames were consuming the door. He raced to one of the barred windows, and used the butt of the rifle to smash the glass in, seeing the troupe huddling together. "Everybody take a mattress!" he yelled. "Hold it in front of you, over your face and head. When I get the door open, you run out one at a time, your mattress in front of you. Nobody's going to be shooting at you." He then turned to the door. The fire was fierce, now, the smoke thick and heavy, but the flames had already burned deeply into the wood. Wrapping his kerchief around his face, he ran to the door, forcing himself to face the furnace that now reached gleefully out to envelope him in searing heat and choking smoke.

Using all the strength of his powerful leg muscles, Fargo kicked at the door where the bolt still lay in place. He half turned, then kicked again and again. The wood, weakened by the flames, splintered and the bolt fell away. "Run, dammit!" Fargo shouted as the flaming door opened. "Run!" He stayed as close as he could to the scorching heat of the flames, seeing the mattress appear in the doorway, half hidden by smoke and flame. One actor stumbled out and Fargo pulled away the mattress, which was already smoldering. He pulled the young woman behind it out and away from the house. A second mattress appeared and he did the same, sending another young woman running from the house. A man came next and again Fargo pulled the mattress from him as the man fell gasping onto the floor. Fargo stayed, enduring the intense heat of the flames, pulling mattress after mattress from each figure that stumbled through the flames and smoke. Finally, they were all outside, the longhouse now thoroughly consumed in flames. He walked to where they all huddled together and Hazel almost leaped into his arms.

"Told you I'd be watching you," he said.

"That was awfully close watching," she protested as she gave him an urgent fiery kiss.

"It's not over. Eakins will be coming by morning. You've got to be someplace far away for a while," he told them.

"How about the caves where you found me. They're plenty big enough and hidden away," Hazel said.

"They'll do," Fargo agreed. "We've eight horses. Some of you can double up. Give me a hand," he said to one of the young men and another joined him.

"I'm Keith," the one introduced himself.

"Jack," the other offered. "Hazel told us what you did before all hell broke loose."

"As I said, it's not over," Fargo answered and the two men helped round up the horses that were tethered behind a small hut at the back of the long bunkhouse. Finding some tins of food, Fargo took them along and swung in behind Hazel. With a few members of the troupe riding two to a horse, they set out through the dark for the high hill country on the far side of the Yellow River. Dawn came up long before they reached the river and the caves. Fargo swore silently. He had wanted to be with Brenda and Harley before the day broke. When they reached the densely overgrown caves, Hazel led the way in. "I'm hoping you won't have to hide out here more than a few days," Fargo told them.

"Can you save Harley?" one of the young women asked.

"That'll depend on timing and Eakins," he said. There was no reason to give them false hope and their faces were shrouded in dismay as he rode away. He kept the Ovaro in tree cover as he retraced his steps. He'd gone halfway back toward town when he saw bands of riders sweeping through the hills, eight to ten riders in each band. Fargo cursed. Eakins had paid his visit to the hostages earlier than Fargo had expected, and he felt apprehension spiral through him. Eakins had found his trump hand gone and he frantically wanted it back. He could imagine the rage that exploded inside the man when he found only the charred remains of the long house. But did it mean that he had returned to Brenda and Harley? Fargo winced at the thought. It was what he'd wanted to prevent happening.

A grimace riding with him, he moved carefully, letting every band of searchers go past him until he reached the low hills. The sun was in the late afternoon sky. He rode, hoping Eakins had sent his men scouring the territory as soon as he'd found his jailhouse burnt to the ground. Eakins was no fool. He could afford to wait to get back to Harley, and finding the troupe would be his first concern. Fargo hoped the bands of searchers was a good sign in a perverse way. It could mean Eakins hadn't rushed back to take it out on Harley and Brenda, that he'd reined in his fury and was being furiously practical with his search parties, refusing to let rage interfere with his objective. As Fargo moved into the lowland and down the road to town he still kept to the cottonwoods. He wanted desperately to get to Brenda and Harley, but he knew he'd never reach them by day. Eakins would have so many men watching the hotel that a fly couldn't get in unseen. He'd have to wait for dark, Fargo knew, and even then it would still be risky. Drawing the pinto deeper into the woods, he dismounted and sat down in the shade of a gambel oak and leaned back against its gray-brown scaly bark.

He dozed, awakening when the night wind came. Returning to the saddle, he continued to keep to the tree cover as much as he could, certain that Eakins would have his searchers roaming through the night. When he reached the town Fargo again approached from the rear, this time dismounting to creep forward on foot. He was within a few yards of the rear of the hotel when he spotted a man standing in the shadows, his eyes on the hotel's rear door. Fargo circled in silent steps, coming up behind him. The man never heard him, collapsing without so much as a grunt as the butt of the Colt came down on his head. Fargo left the unconscious man where he was and hurried through the rear door of the hotel. He started down the hall-way, but suddenly flattened himself against the wall when he saw a lone guard standing in front of the door to Brenda's room.

Fargo swore silently. There were probably others not too far away. Noise could bring them running. Shots certainly would. He stood frozen in place when the door to one of the other rooms a few feet down from him opened. A middle-aged woman came out, locked the door, and started down the hall. Fargo was at her side in a second, tossing her a reassuring smile as she glanced at him, puzzled. He walked a pace behind her, close enough to appear as if he was with her. The guard gave them only a casual glance as they came abreast of him, plainly not on the lookout for a couple. As the woman went on, Fargo halted and whirled, and a split second later, the barrel of the Colt was pushing into the man's stomach.

"One shout and it's your last one," Fargo hissed. The guard, his eyes wide with fear, licked his lips and nodded. With his left hand, Fargo reached around him, turned the doorknob, and pushed the man into the room. Once inside, he pulled the Colt away from the man's stomach and smashed it onto his head. The guard collapsed in a heap. Turning, Fargo saw only Harley inside the room. "Where's Brenda?" he asked.

Harley, recovering from his surprise, pushed to his feet. "Gone with Eakins," he said.

"Why?" Fargo bit out, alarm pushing at him at once.

"Eakins came here. He was in a rage. He cursed you out, said he was going to find you and kill you where you stood. Everybody else, too. I didn't know what he meant," Harley said.

"He meant your troupe. He found out they had escaped. I got everyone out, including Hazel," Fargo said.

"Oh, God, oh, God, what wonderful news!" Harley shouted and clapped his hands.

"But you didn't know that then. Did you give him what he wanted?" Fargo frowned.

"I would have. You know I'd decided I had to," Harley said. "But Brenda jumped up. She said she could help him find you. Fargo, I couldn't believe my ears. I asked her why she was doing that, but she told me to shut up. She asked Eakins to take her with him and he did. I'm still in shock at her doing that. Why would she? My God, why?"

"Good question." Fargo frowned as thoughts raced through his mind. Had she been trying to curry favor with Eakins to save her own skin? he wondered. He had come to know Brenda. Her surface reasons were never the real ones. As his mind continued to swirl in thought, the terrible possibility rose up before him and his eyes went to Harley. "Harley, did you give Brenda those clues Eakins wanted from you?" he asked with a sinking feeling in his stomach.

Harley looked faintly uncomfortable with his shrug. "Yes. It seemed like the right thing to do," he said.

"Why, dammit?" Fargo barked.

"I was going to give them to him anyway to save the others. You know I'd decided that," Harley said.

"So why didn't you just do that when the time came?" Fargo pressed.

"Brenda told me she was sure she could still work out a deal with Eakins. She said I owed it to everyone to let her try," Harley said. "But she needed the clues to do it, of course. She persuaded me to let her try for the sake of everyone."

"Brenda doesn't give a shit about any of you," Fargo threw at him. "She wanted another try at working out the deal she'd already made with Eakins."

"She's already made a deal with him?" Harley asked, aghast.

"That's right. Damn her little two-faced soul! Getting the clues from you was her only chance left to deal with Eakins before you did," Fargo said.

"But you changed all that," Harley said.

"Only she was ready, thanks to you. She jumped in with that offer to help him find me. That was a smokescreen for you, in case she'd still need you. Brenda plays every angle," Fargo said.

Harley put his hands to his face. "After all this, after everything, Eakins has what he wants. He can go ahead with whatever he's planned on doing." He groaned.

Fargo swore bitterly, Harley's words all too true. Eakins would win. He had all his men ready and poised. By now he'd called off his search parties. He didn't need the troupe now. He didn't need any pressure on Harley any longer. He had everything he wanted, thanks to Brenda's self-serving duplicity. Fargo's fist slammed into his palm. He'd not let Eakins win, not without a hell of a fight. But he had to see

Brenda, first. Fargo felt certain that by now, she had learned the truth of everything he'd told her. By now she had learned about dealing with the devil.

And by now Eakins would have bragged to her, told her of his plans. It was in his nature to gloat. Fargo whirled and pulled the door open. "Stay here. It's the safest place for you," he told Harley and hurried from the room. He ran back out the rear door and vaulted onto the Ovaro. It was time to end things. As he rode, he grew certain of one thing: Eakins would be even more ruthless as he saw triumph in his grasp. Fargo would have to match ruthlessness with ruthlessness, and he began to form his own plans.

7

A midnight moon hung high as Fargo neared the Eakins place. He left the Ovaro in the cottonwoods and crept forward on foot. Lamps were burning brightly all around the front of the house and at the bunkhouse, the yard, and the corrals. He saw the horses hitched to the big drays with the chain-linked stake sides, both loaded with prospecting tools that included cradles and Long Toms. Men were adding still more equipment, such as shovels, pickaxes, sluice pans. He spied Eakins moving among his gunhands, who were now all gathered together in one corral. Close to a hundred and fifty gunhands, he guessed. Preparations were being made to leave soon, Fargo decided. It was plain to see that Eakins wanted everything and everyone in place by morning.

Fargo searched for Brenda but she was nowhere to be seen. He wasn't surprised, and his eyes traveled across the scene again. In a way, it made his immediate task easier. Everyone was preoccupied, the focus of all attention on preparations to move out. He doubted that there were a half-dozen men on sentry duty. Moving quickly in the trees, Fargo made his way to the rear of the main house. He was glad to see it was still relatively dark, all the lamps at the front of the house and the corrals. With quick, purposeful movements, he cut across the open ground to the rear of the house. After all, this was not his first visit here, and he halted at the same window where he'd entered before. He lifted it, and again it slid open. He crawled through into a half-lit hallway.

The house was silent. The only sound came from the activity outside. He hurried forward, and peered into rooms that led from the hallway, finding a study, a dining room, a parlor, a kitchen, three bedrooms, and another parlor. He'd been certain Brenda was here but he began to wonder if Eakins was keeping her somewhere else. He was moving through the halls when he halted at a narrow closed door cut into a back wall, the face of it appearing almost exactly like the wall. He turned the small knob and the door opened. Steps led down, and the glow of a candle flickered up from the bottom of the steps.

Closing the door behind him, Fargo started down the steps. At the bottom, a basement spread out in front of him. At first he saw only boxes, crates, barrels, two old wheelbarrows. Then, peering through the clutter he saw the chair with a figure in it, hands and feet bound to the chair. "Oh, God . . . here, over here," he heard the figure call and recognized Brenda's voice at once. He almost strolled to her, his eyes surveying her.

"Now, that doesn't seem how partners ought to treat each other," he remarked.

Brenda's eyes flashed at him, then the opaque veil dropped over her orbs at once. "You were right about him. I was wrong. Now untie me, dammit," she snapped.

"Admission without contrition. That doesn't do it, honey," Fargo said blandly.

"I'll be contrite later. I promise. Now untie me!" Brenda threw back.

"Not so fast. I want some answers, first," Fargo said.

"All right, then, ask," she muttered.

"What's he going to do?" Fargo queried.

"Find the vein and start working it," she said.

"And all those gunhands?"

"They're going to stake out the river on both sides. He knows others, especially prospectors, will come around as soon as his men starting working the vein. They come, and they can back off alive or get carried away dead. That'll hold for anybody who tries working the vein or the river," Brenda said.

"He going to start in the morning?"

"That's right. He wants everything in place tonight, his gunhands positioned to make everything his."

"Only he's got no more right to do that than anybody else. Nobody can claim public land."

"The most guns make the most right and he's got the most guns," Brenda said almost admiringly.

"How long does he figure to keep this up?" Fargo asked.

"Until he's cleaned out the vein. There's no one to stop him, not with all those gunhands he's got," Brenda said.

"There might be a way," Fargo said.

"Sure, you're just going to snap your fingers and make a hundred and fifty gunhands appear," Brenda said with a sneer.

"Something like that," he said. She peered at him as if he may have lost his senses. "I'll have to get at it," Fargo said. "See you soon."

"Come back here, dammit! You said you'd untie me after you got some answers. I gave you answers," Brenda flared.

"I didn't say how *long* after," Fargo said as he hurried from the basement.

"Son of a bitch, come back here!" Brenda shouted, but he was at the top step already, carefully pushing the door open, then closing it. The sound of Brenda's shouts were abruptly cut off and Fargo ran down the hall to the rear window, crawled outside, and darted across the open land to the trees. He saw a slow movement below as the big drays began to leave the corral, with others falling in behind them. Fargo took the Ovaro and, staying in the cottonwoods, rode away. His would be a much longer trip, and he wanted to be there at sunrise. In some instances, a sign was made of little but appearances. He wanted to create as good a one as he could, and he put the horse into a trot. But as he rode in the loneliness of the night, he disliked the pictures that came to him.

They reminded him that he, no less than anyone else, was a product of his world, his community, or his surroundings, and these fundamental truths were not easy to turn his back on. He saw the massacred men, women, and children at the Conestoga, each riddled with Shoshoni arrows. He saw the savagery of the attack on Jed Hopper's little group of settlers, an attack that failed only for the surprise he'd arranged for the attackers. And he knew that there'd be more Shoshoni attacks in the future. His warning to Brenda came back to stab at him. *Deals with the devil usually work out for the devil.*

Wasn't that what he was about to do? he asked himself. But he turned the question away in anger. He wasn't *seeking* a deal with the devil. He had no choice. It was the only option open to him. Sometimes you have to fight fire with fire, open a dam to prevent a greater flood. He was going to do the only thing he could do to stop a ruthless, greedy killer. None of those with Eakins was free from guilt. They had killed for him, for his money, and they were willing to do more of it. There was a price for working for the devil. Fargo would make sure they paid it.

But as the night hours rolled on, Fargo knew the sourness inside him would stay. Despite all he'd told himself, it would not go away. There was a price for rationalization, too. He could only ask forgiveness from all those who would not understand. He rode on and the night still held the land when he reached the Shoshoni camp. He walked the pinto almost to the edge of the teepees before sliding to the ground. The first fingers of dawn were beginning to touch the sky as he stole into the camp, past figures sleeping on the ground. He picked his way to the chief's decorated teepee and halted. Standing very straight and very still, he waited and watched the sun start to define the land's shapes and forms with light. He heard the sound of waking from behind him, then short gasps of surprise and more voices raised, a strong murmur rising. He remained motionless and the flap of the teepee flew open. The tall, bare-chested figure stepped out, his piercing eyes finding Fargo at once. Fargo continued to stay still, even as he saw Awenita approaching out of the corner of his eye.

The entire camp was awake, now, filled with murmured exchanges. The Shoshoni chief's eyes continued to stay on him but Fargo caught a flash of something behind his intense glare, and he hoped the thoughts he wanted to plant in the Indian's mind had borne fruit. No ordinary man penetrated the Shoshoni camp without being detected. Had the Great Spirits aided this white man? Was Fargo's coming a sign? Fargo hoped those things had come into the chief's mind. As Awenita stepped forward, the chief spoke and she translated, her eyes on Fargo. "Why have you returned to the Shoshoni camp?"

"Those who attacked you and Cholena have come back," Fargo said. Wamblee's face hardened as Awenita explained. "They have brought many more. It will take all of your warriors to fight them," Fargo said.

"Where?" the chief asked through Awenita.

"The river that runs through the low hills. They have come to take it as theirs," Fargo said.

Wamblee's eyes grew more piercing. "Why do you come to tell me this?" he questioned.

"I know the chief of the Shoshoni will not rest until this dishonor is made right," Fargo said.

"That is so," Awenita translated. "But my father asks if this is all in your heart."

Fargo grunted, allowing a half smile. The Shoshoni was as canny as he was fierce. "It will be a terrible battle and a great victory. Maybe, with such a great victory, the Shoshoni can stop attacking small wagons and homes. Who needs to slay field mice when they have slain bears?" Fargo said.

The chief thought for a moment, then finally answered. "Perhaps," Awenita said, translating the single word. Fargo nodded, happy to get a half promise. The chief turned, then strolled among his warriors. He spoke with quick, firm animation coloring his voice. In moments, the camp was alive with preparations for battle. Ponies were brought out, warpaint applied to their coats, arrows put into hide quivers, rifles checked by those who had them, amulets of magical strength wrapped around necks and wrists. Awenita came beside Fargo, her voice low.

"This will be another debt to you," she said. "It is not right. I have not honored the first one. I must. I want to. And not just for debt."

Fargo touched her hand unobtrusively. "You will. When this is done. I want that, too," he said. Her fingers moved inside his palm, a message without words. He released her hand as the chief approached to speak with her.

"My father says you will ride with them, fight with them," Awenita told him.

Fargo smiled inwardly. He had been given a challenge. His answer would decide his fate. The Shoshoni chief withheld his trust. He'd not let himself be tricked. He wanted the white man's words made into deeds. Fargo nodded and walked to where he'd left the Ovaro. He was in the saddle when he returned and swung alongside the chief. With a wave of one arm, the chief sent his warriors forward and Fargo glanced back, estimating that there were close to a hundred and fifty braves. Wamblee led the way down into the low hills but kept in the trees, and Fargo marveled at how silent so many ponies and riders could be. When the Yellow River came into sight, Fargo saw the Shoshoni shift into single file.

The chief continued to parallel the river below as he stayed in the trees until he suddenly halted. Fargo saw the scene below and a dozen yards ahead. Eakins and his prospectors were exploring and working in six different places, erecting sluices and Long Toms at each place. The sound of pickaxes biting into rock came from behind the trees. Fargo's eyes sought out the gunhands, seeing that they had been placed in a double line stretching nearly a thousand yards on both sides of the river. Eakins plainly wanted an impressive show that would certainly dissuade any small prospectors from joining in the mining. Any larger outfits he'd take care of with bullets. He had established a zone for his mining operation and to hell with anyone and everyone.

But as Fargo's eyes scanned the scene, he saw that they had given the Shoshoni a real opportunity. They were thinly spread out all the way down the line. Fargo glanced at the chief. Wamblee had seen the same thing and was busy talking to his braves. Unable to understand his words, Fargo had no trouble understanding his hand motions. He watched as about half the braves formed three groups, thirty braves in each. The rest stayed back in the trees. At the chief's signal, the three bands burst from the trees and raced down to the river. Wamblee led the first group, his glance at Fargo unmistakable in meaning. Fargo nodded and put the Ovaro into a gallop alongside the chief. The three groups hurtled into Eakins's surprised gunhands with devastating effect, ripping gaping holes into their lines. Fargo fired as he raced beside the chief, bringing down two of the gunhands who were trying to regroup by dropping to their knees in order to form knots of firepower.

But Fargo saw the fury of the Shoshoni attack, as Eakins's gunhands fell to arrows, rifle fire, tomahawks, spears, and knives. One man, escaping the initial attack, saw Fargo and charged his horse at him. "Stinkin' son of a bitch!" he shouted as he emptied his six-gun. But Fargo had dropped low in the saddle and the man's shots were wild, all fury and no aim. Fargo's single answering shot hit its mark and the man doubled up in the saddle before he fell. Fargo spun the Ovaro, and found Sam Eakins on a rise near one of the sluices, screaming orders at his men.

Those on both ends rallied from their initial surprise. They began to charge in from both ends, their objective to trap the three Shoshoni groups between them in a hail of cross fire. The countermaneuver was tactically sound. It would have worked but for the main force of the Shoshoni who just then charged down out of the hills. In moments, the course of the battle had changed again, and all of the gunhands were now fighting desperately to regroup. But they were no cavalry troop trained at battlefield reorganization. They were a collection of hired guns who knew only barroom shoot-outs, facing fierce Shoshoni warriors with skill and experience. In only minutes, they were reduced to fighting in little desperate pockets. Fargo rode forward, and caught motion to his right, seeing two of the gunhands charging at him, rifles raised to fire. Fargo twisted his body as he dived from the saddle, feeling a bullet graze his cheek.

"Goddamn bastard. Kill him!" he heard one shout as Fargo hit the ground, rolled, and came up on one knee. The two riflemen had charged past and now it took them precious seconds to rein up, turn their horses around, and charge again. Fargo fired from one knee and the nearest rider bounced in the saddle before he fell from his mount. The second one had his rifle raised to fire again when Fargo's bullet slammed into him an inch from where he held the rifle to his shoulder. The gunhand reared backward, the rifle sailing into the air, and Fargo saw the spray of scarlet from his collarbone as he fell backward off his mount.

Pushing to his feet with a shrill whistle, Fargo retrieved the Ovaro and swung into the saddle. Eakins's men were still battling as best they could. They had no dedication or loyalty, Fargo realized. Fighting simply meant a chance at staying alive a little longer. Fargo's eyes swept the scene, from the low hills to the other side of the river that now was more red than yellow. Some of the gunhands were escaping on horseback, others straggling along on foot. The Shoshoni were either still fighting or tending to their wounded. Fargo almost missed the burly figure streaking into the trees on a horse, his fancy vest ripped and streaked with blood. Sending the Ovaro into a gallop, Fargo charged across the river onto the other side, jumping the horse over clusters of dead bodies and racing into the hills.

The shouts and gunfire grew muted at once, the hills acting as a green curtain. Fargo strained his ears, picking up the sounds of the horse ahead of him. The man was fleeing, saving only himself. That meant he'd return another time to take up where he'd left off, another excursion into ruthless greed. Fargo spurred the Ovaro forward and finally glimpsed Eakins moving through the forest some twenty yards ahead of him. Whether by sixth sense or hearing, Eakins knew he was being followed, and he turned in the saddle and saw Fargo. He raised a big Remington Beals army revolver, a six-shot, single-action weapon with an eight-inch barrel, a gun that was as accurate as it was powerful. Eakins held his fire to get a better shot, as Fargo spurred the pinto behind two alders and edged closer to the man.

Suddenly he heard a sound only a few feet to his

right. Fargo threw a glance in time to see one of the gunhands rise from a thick clump of brush. The man's face was cut and bruised, his clothes stained with blood. He stared at Fargo with eyes dull with pain and shock. He moved one hand up and Fargo saw the six-gun in his quivering hand. "Goddamn Indian lover," the man rasped, swaying as he bit out the words. At another time the accusation might have stung, and might have elicited a response. The man's finger pressed the trigger, two shots too close to miss.

Fargo felt one bullet graze his shoulder, the other his bicep, and knew he was falling from the saddle. Somehow, he caught a glimpse of the gunhand as the man collapsed in a heap. Fargo struck the ground hard and the shock snapped away the film that had begun to fall over his eyes. He felt the trickle of blood seeping down his temple, his eyes fogging over again. He shook his head hard to clear it, and felt his vision returning just in time to glimpse Sam Eakins charging down at him. The man kicked out with one foot, catching Fargo on the shoulder. Fargo flew a half-dozen feet. The curtain tried to come over his eyes again and he rolled, wincing at the pain in his shoulder as he continued to shake his head clear. The curtain parted slightly but stayed fuzzy. Fargo rolled across the ground, only to strike his head against a tree trunk. Once again the shock cleared his vision.

Sam Eakins was now standing over him with a length of branch in one hand. He swung it, smashing it into Fargo's side, and Fargo felt the wave of pain shoot through him. "I ain't gonna kill you, Fargo. That'd be too good for you. I'm goin' to bust you up so you won't ever run again, walk again, wave your arms again, or screw again," he heard Eakins roar, seeing him raise the length of wood with both hands this time. He started to bring it crashing down on Fargo's knee when Fargo managed to roll aside. The blow smashed into the ground with a thud, and Fargo wrapped his arms around the burly man's leg. He pulled with all the strength still in his body and Eakins lost his balance and went down on one knee.

Fargo threw a left hook from an almost prone position. It had just enough power to make Eakins topple backward. With sharp pain coursing through his body, Fargo pushed himself up just enough to throw a right. It caught Sam Eakins on the side of the jaw but not with enough power. Eakins shook it off, and kicked out with one powerful leg. The blow caught Fargo in his abdomen. Fargo pitched forward, the pain racking his entire body. He gasped, each gasp an exercise in gut-wrenching pain. When he managed to look up, he saw Sam Eakins standing before him, the length of wood raised up in both hands once again. "Your spine, this time, you bastard," Eakins roared. Fargo wanted to roll but found he couldn't. His abdominal muscles were cramped, holding him as in a vise. He could only stare up at Sam Eakins and the club that was going to destroy his spine. Suddenly, he saw Sam Eakins's jaw drop, and his mouth fall open. A stream of blood poured from his lips and his eyes rolled back in his head. It was only then that Fargo saw the flint arrowhead protruding from the middle of the man's chest.

The length of wood fell from Sam Eakins's grip and the man's burly body seemed to collapse in on itself as he sank to the ground. Fargo's eyes went past his fallen form to see the Shoshoni chief on his pony, still holding his bow up in shooting position.

Slowly, he lowered it and slid from his pony. Crying out in pain, Fargo managed to pull himself to his feet as he fought for breath. He met the chief's deep-set eyes and spoke, using sign language to help him with his words.

"Honor is done, exchanged," Fargo said, making the sign for exchange and for honor. The chief took a moment in thought but finally nodded and pointed to the Ovaro.

Fargo winced as he pulled himself onto the horse, and kept the pinto at a walk as he followed Wamblee. Near the river, the warriors were gathered with their wounded and dead, and soon took up to follow their chief. To Fargo, the trip to the Shoshoni camp had never been so long. Awenita was first among those who hurried to aid the returning warriors. She went to Fargo and helped him from the pinto. "You will come to my teepee," she said and he was happy to follow her. Inside the tent, he lay down on a bearskin rug. "Stay," she said and hurried away to return with a stone vessel filled with ephedra tea and a small stone dish containing an ointment paste. He sipped the tea, finding it sharp and invigorating, as Awenita proceeded to take most of his clothes off.

"I can't stay," he told her. She ignored the statement as she began to rub the ointment into his strained abdomen, back, legs, and torso. "Feels good. What is it?" He asked.

"White willow bark and wintergreen," Awenita said, her touch firm and arm. "My father understands what you said, Fargo," she added.

"I hoped so," Fargo said.

"But what of my debt? It still waits. I have not honored it," she said.

"When I come again. My word," he said. She let her hands play across his body, continuing even when she had no more ointment to apply. He saw her eyes enjoy his muscled smoothness, her lips slightly parted as she massaged his body. Hidden beneath the elkskin garment, she exuded a definite sensuality. When night fell, Fargo rose and dressed, the ointment already soothing his aching muscles. Awenita stood very close to him. "Very soon, Little Deer," he said and realized he wanted very much to come back.

"I will wait. My father will ask about it. I will tell him your word," Awenita said.

"Tell him to remember my other words," Fargo said.

"Which words?" she asked.

"The words of mice and bears," Fargo said and hurried from the teepee. It was not much of a message, he realized, yet if the Shoshoni chief agreed with it, some real good had come out of all this. He rode slowly, his body burning despite the ointment. He made his way through the night, finally reaching town and the hotel. Harley leaped to his feet when he entered the room.

"God, it's a relief to see you, Fargo! What's happened? I'm biting my nails down to nothing," Harley said.

"Eakins is dead. Most of his men, too. The Shoshoni attacked while they were at the river," Fargo said.

Harley gave him a sidelong glance. "Just at the right time?"

"You never know when an Indian attack will come," Fargo said blandly.

"Amazing timing for us," Harley said.

"Never look a gift attack in the mouth," Fargo admonished.

"Wouldn't think of it," Harley said. "What's happened to Brenda?"

"She found out that her deals were off with Eakins," he said and told him everything Brenda had tried to do. When he finished, Cousin Harley's soft face was more sad than angry.

"What about the troupe?" he asked.

"I'll get them in the morning," Fargo said. Harley peered at him.

"I want to go on. Will you help me find the gold vein? I know you've done so much. Could you see your way to doing a little more?" he said.

"I never like leaving things unfinished," Fargo replied.

"Oh, thank you, thank you! I hope we can make it up to you someway, certainly with part of the gold when you find it," Harley said.

"Right now I'll get Brenda. She'll be your problem," Fargo said.

"I won't let her be," Harley said. "From what I saw her do, and the things you told me, Brenda isn't the person I once knew. I won't be taken in by her again." Fargo nodded and hurried from the room. Outside, he rode from town and when he reached the Eakins place he found it deserted. Anyone who'd survived the battle had fled. Bunkhouse doors hung open, equipment was left on the ground, a lone lamp was left lighting the barn, and only a half-dozen horses remained in the corral. Fargo stopped at the main house and went inside, pausing at the silence before he made his way to the basement. The candle still glowed at the bottom of the steps.

"In here, Jesus . . . in here, whoever you are!" Brenda called out when she heard the basement door open. Fargo stepped forward into the candlelight. "You! It's about time, dammit!" she flung at him as he untied her.

"Had things to do. You know what's happened?" he asked as she rubbed circulation back into her wrists and ankles.

"No. I heard some shouting and horses galloping away," she said.

"It's all done. Eakins's operation is over," Fargo said.

Brenda's pale blue eyes stared at him in disbelief. "You found the gunhands to fight him?" she breathed.

"Kind of," Fargo said. "You're over, too, Brenda."

"Nonsense." She huffed and rose to her feet.

"Harley's onto you," Fargo said.

"Don't bet on it," Brenda said. "Harley wouldn't listen to you. He won't believe you."

"No, he'll believe himself. His own instincts will kick in," Fargo said and met her stare. "Whatever happened to that will your Uncle Charles had, the one that said you and Harley have to share everything together? Seems to me you decided to hell with it," he said.

"It was becoming a burden." She sniffed, then took a step closer. Her wan azure eyes softened. "When will I see you again?" she asked.

"Can't say." He shrugged. "I quit, in case I forgot to mention it. Some while back, when I realized you were all sentiment and caring. It was too much for me," he said sarcastically.

Brenda's eyes narrowed at him. "Seems to me you enjoyed that night in bed. Didn't find any fault then," she said.

He smiled. "It's easy to be fooled in bed. Happens all the time."

"Go to hell, Fargo," Brenda said as he started up the stairs. She hurried after him and he gestured to one of the horses in the corral.

"Pick one for yourself," he said and was in the saddle, riding away before she found a horse to mount. He turned the Ovaro onto the road from town and headed north to the high hills. Brenda would make Harley her first visit, he was certain. But she'd fail to manipulate him. He felt certain of that, too. Harley wasn't the mark she thought he was. Cousin Harley's softness was deceptive. He was a dreamer without being a fool and he had an iron integrity. He'd proven that. Brenda would learn it again. She'd come in greed. She'd leave in need.

The new day had dawned when Fargo reached the caves and the hills shook with cheers. Hazel rode beside him all the way back to the hotel, where another joyous reunion erupted. In a little while, Harley took him aside and anticipated his question. "Brenda was here but she left to wait for the next stage East. Didn't like my answers, I'm afraid."

"She's your cousin. You were close. You had trust and faith in her. It has to hurt you a little," Fargo said.

Harley's smile was wry. " 'In this harsh world, draw thy breath in pain.' *Hamlet,*" he said. "The world goes on, however. Can you find that gold vein, Fargo?"

"It'll take the town burial crew a day to clean up the hills. Anyway, I can't start looking till the day after. I have some things to take care of first."

"Dinner tonight, then," Harley said and Fargo nodded. He couldn't blame Harley and the others for feeling confident. They had been to the edge of death and survived. Their dreams still lived, too. He'd try to make them come true.

8

Fargo stretched out on his bedroll, gazing out to the deep, dark bulk of the Salmon River Range. It would be good with Little Deer, he pondered, simple, uncomplicated, with no hidden motives. He found himself looking forward to that moment. He had learned the sensual power in simplicity.

A face swam into his mind, pretty, sweet, yet with its own eager demands. Hazel had wanted to spend the night with him but he'd convinced her to stay at the hotel with the others. She had never been part of Brenda's scheming beauty, nor her greed. But she had been a part of all that had happened, all the tortuous turns and twists, and he'd had enough of all of it. He'd promised to try and find Harley's lode and then he'd close this sorry chapter. He drew his eyes shut and told himself he'd not let Brenda's pale blue eyes intrude on his dreams. But as he slept, he learned one more lesson. Dreams did not obey orders.

Fargo did manage to sleep through the night, though, and the morning sun was full and warm when he peered down at the Yellow River, running yellow once again. Beyond the far shore, the rocks rose up into the hills, the grass still streaked with scarlet. Harley had given him the clues and now he let them run through his mind again. The old prospector had been cryptic, anxious to protect his find even when he confided in Harley. Two phrases formed the first clue:

> *Crowns Above—Gold Below*
> He'd used only three words for the second:
> *Only The Heart*
> Three more words provided the last:
> *A Road Unseen*

Fargo sent the pinto down to the riverbank and across the river as he surveyed what Eakins's prospectors had begun. They had immediately begun chopping into the front row of the tall rocks, probably because they were closest to the river, and there were little flecks of yellow visible along the base of each rock. The flecks were enough to satisfy Eakins that there was gold below. Fargo also saw other marks on the rocks, old and worn, where previous prospectors had put their axes to the rocks. None of the marks cut in very deeply, he noted as he rode on, climbing to the next line of tall rocks well back of those closest to the river.

He didn't search for marks near the base but concentrated his search at the tops of the rocks that formed a good part of the hills. Slowly, he peered at each rock formation with no regard to their closeness to the river. As he rode, he saw that the tops of some rocks were covered with black lichen, some rimmed with blue gentian, others with cinquefoil. Still others were covered with alpine sandwort, some with yellow and orange lichens. Turning, he rode back along the next line of rocks, again examining the very tops of each formation when he suddenly pulled to a halt. He stared at the blossoms that covered the tall rocks ahead, strong green leaves with small, rounded, pale-pink-colored flowers. The name came to him after a moment searching his memory. "Rosecrowns," he muttered softly, letting a laugh of satisfaction escape him and turned the pinto down along the edge of the rock.

He could just about see the river when he reached the base of the rock but its distance didn't bother him. Instead, he let another laugh form inside him as the old prospector's second clue came to mind. Dismounting, he used the few pickaxes, shovels, and spades he'd brought along with him and began to dig into the soil at the side of the tall rock. He dug hard, turning up earth alongside the rock, pausing every few feet to dig his hands into the newly turned ground and then continuing on again. He had dug for more than an hour, a tall pyramid of earth growing beside him when he finally paused to dig his hands into the freshly unearthed soil against the edge of the rock. He probed with his fingers, clawed some more, and suddenly a half shout of triumph burst from him.

He had just pulled his hands back when he heard another shout from the river. Pushing to his feet, Fargo stepped around the tall pyramid of earth he'd dug, moving out to where he was in the clear. He waved at Harley and six members of his troupe on the far bank, all carrying prospecting tools. He had almost forgotten that he'd arranged with Harley to give him a few hours head start and then meet him at the river. He waved and called back, waiting while Harley and the others crossed the river and made their way to where he stood beside the mound of earth. He pointed to the tall rock. "Your gold is in there," he said simply.

"How do you know?" Harley asked eagerly. "You deciphered Crazy George's clues?"

"They were more tricky than hard and, as with most clues, once you unravel one, the others begin to fall into place," Fargo said. "The top of every one of these rocks is thickly overgrown with different vegetation. This one is covered with a hardy bloom called rose-crown. Crowns above . . . gold below."

Harley stared back. "But it can't be. It's too far back from the river. The vein we want has to be in one of the rocks near the river for all that gold sediment to wash into the water."

"Lots of others thought that and didn't come up with anything," Fargo said and dug his hands into the soil beside the rock. "Feel this," he said and Harley dug hands into the newly dug earth.

"It's moist," he said.

"Bull's-eye," Fargo said. "There's an underground stream that flows through this rock. It's not uncommon. They're fed by deep, underground springs. The stream goes deep into the ground, under all the other rocks, and empties into the river."

Harley's mouth hung open as he breathed the words. "A road unseen. The second clue."

"Bull's-eye again." Fargo nodded.

"The third clue?" Harley asked.

"Your lode is very deep inside the rock. Ordinary surface drilling wouldn't find it and that's what most prospectors do. They all thought it was too far back from the river and surface drilling didn't show anything. Crazy George's love for chasing down places others had rejected finally paid off."

"My God," Harley said, staring in silence for a moment. Then he spun around. "Keith, get the others. Have them bring more tools. We'll need everyone on this," he said. The young man raced back across the river and Fargo joined with the others as they started to strike pickaxes into the rock. They had made only a small dent in the unyielding stone when Keith returned with the others. More hands and more pickaxes helped dig deeper into the solid rock, but night came before they had chopped away enough to find anything but more rock.

"Post guards. Six of them, in shifts," Fargo told Harley.

"You expect trouble?" Harley frowned.

"No, not really. But someone may have watched us. Word travels fast," Fargo said. "Just taking precautions. People do things they wouldn't normally do over gold."

"I feel like Eakins and I don't like it," Harley said, his soft face troubled.

"You're not. You've a right to protect your find. You're not out to kill anyone who wants to hunt for their own vein. That's what Eakins was all about," Fargo said. Harley nodded, then posted the sentry shifts. Fargo found his own spot to lay down his bedroll, higher on the hillside. He'd just undressed when Hazel appeared. She knelt down beside him.

"I'm too exhausted to do what I want to do," she said.

"Me too," he lied gently.

"There'll be plenty of time," she said and he nodded in agreement. She kissed him and trudged away. He lay back and realized again that he wanted only to finish things here and be gone. Greed, deceit, and betrayal leave a bitter legacy. He grimaced. It spread like an infection, over the blameless as well as the guilty. Pulling sleep to him, he woke with the new day and worked hard beside everyone else. By late afternoon, they had dug deep and he was beginning to have misgivings when one of the troupe let out a shout that brought everyone running. Fargo stared at the yellow vein that ran through the rock for a long while until finally finding his voice.

"Start digging it out. You can take some rock, too. We'll separate the gold after it's dug out," he said and joined in as everyone attacked the vein. The pieces they dug out were put into a pile and as the day began to draw to a close, Fargo sat down and chopped the gold free of surrounding rocks, examining each piece.

"Everyone's too drained to go on," Harley said as the day ended. Fargo nodded and rose, took a last glance at the pieces of gold in the rocks, then brought his bedroll under a juniper. He slept quickly and woke with the first light of dawn. He returned to the piece of rock, stared at the brassy, light yellow color and ran his fingertips over the ore. As the others gathered around munching on hard biscuits, he extracted two pieces out of the surrounding ore as the others looked on. "We'll start separating after we've collected more," Harley said.

Fargo made no reply as he smashed them against each other. "What are you doing?" Harley gasped in alarm. Fargo smashed the two pieces together again, harder, this time. They broke into dozens of little pieces that fell from his hands to scatter on the ground. Harley and the others stared, their mouths open as Fargo glanced up at them. His own face held a grim sorrow in it.

"Pyrite," he said, letting the word drop from his lips with distaste.

"Pyrite?" Harley echoed.

"Also called fool's gold," Fargo said.

They stared at him until Haley broke the silence. "How do you know? How can you tell?" he questioned.

"Real gold wouldn't have shattered like that. Real gold would have flattened out," Fargo said. They continued to stare at him. "There are other tests, like boiling a piece in a soap kettle laced with lye and baking soda, then treating it with nitric acid. It changes the color and texture of pyrite, but has no effect on real gold. The test I just did never fails."

Harley stared up at the rock veined with yellow. "You saying none of this is gold?" he asked.

"That's right. I was bothered by the brassy yellow in the color. Crazy George found himself a rich vein of pyrite. He's not the first to have done that. It's an easy mistake to make. Of course, if he'd gotten to digging it out and testing it at an assayer's, he'd have found out. But he never got around to that."

"He just got around to telling me," Harley moaned.

"The vein has been leaking pyrite into the river, not gold. That can happen, too. Not often, but it can," Fargo said. "Yellow is yellow, but not necessarily gold."

Harley put his hands to his face, finally drawing them away after a few minutes. "All a waste. People killed. A town made to disappear. Everything meaningless, all for nothing."

"Not exactly," Fargo said. "An evil man is gone. The town and everyone in or near it will be a better place for that."

"Yes, probably," Harley agreed. "But all our plans, our hopes, they're gone, vanished just like Grange."

"Why?" Fargo pushed at him and Harley stared back with a gathering frown. "You have your gold. Right in front of you," Fargo said.

Harley's frown deepened. "What are you saying?

"Your gold is what you are, what brought you out here in the first place. Your gold is your talents, your abilities, the things you can bring people. Stories, entertainment, food for the mind and the spirit—all those things you said the old Greeks and Shakespeare brought to their people. That's your gold. That's what it's always been and it's still yours."

A slow smile began to edge Harley's lips. "Yes, of course," he murmured. His voice growing stronger, he repeated himself, "Yes, of course!" He looked at the others and they murmured in agreement. Harley brought his eyes back to Fargo. "Thanks for reminding us," he said. "It's easy to get carried away, forgetting what you have for what you don't have."

"Pyrite's not gold but it's not worthless. You can get a price for it, enough to build that new theater you want," Fargo said.

"Yes, yes!" someone else shouted. "Let's keep digging, and get what we can out of all this."

"We'll get our new theater out of it," Harley said. "No riches, not for any of us, but what we most want. Our own gold, as you put it, Fargo. We might even change the name to the Pyrite Pioneer Players."

"There you go." Fargo laughed.

Harley thrust his hand out. "Thanks for everything, Fargo. There's no gold to pay you. We can only say thanks. It's all we can give you."

"How about two tickets to your first performance

in your new theater?" Fargo said and received a shot of enthusiasm. "I'll be moving on, now. Keep digging," he said and found Hazel beside him as he walked toward the Ovaro.

"I thought you might stay on." She half pouted.

"Another time, another day. Nothing to do with you," Fargo told her.

"I'll be here when you come back for those tickets," she said, clinging to him.

"Good," he said, and let their kiss linger before he crossed the Yellow River. He rode through the town, and sent the Ovaro northward, toward the Salmon River Mountains and into the heart of Shoshoni country. He rode slowly, pausing to wash in a small lake before moving on. The day was nearing a close when he reached the Shoshoni camp. Awenita saw him as he rode in and there were no words needed as her deep, dark brown eyes held his. After he dismounted, she beckoned to him.

She led him into her teepee, then slowly began to remove his clothes, starting with his shirt, running her hands across the rippled muscles of his chest. When he lay naked on the bearskin rug, she whipped the elkskin dress from her and he smiled at her loveliness, every part of her in tune with every other part, her coppery skinned beauty alluring and exotic. He half smiled to himself as he realized the strangeness of it all, of his being there.

He had left the deceit, greed, and betrayal of his own people with their brand of savagery, to come into the midst of a people whose savagery was unmatched. Incongruousness had reached new heights. Yet he felt strangely at peace. Perhaps there was a kind of peace in the simplicity of savagery, of emotions governed only by the basic drives. Only the simplicity of emotions, honest in hate, friendship, passions. That's what had brought him here now, not the insurance of a debt he held.

The faint odor of wintergreen drifted to his nostrils as her touch caressed his skin. Her mouth opened and pressed against his, soft, yet stirring with eagerness. No words were spoken, only a purring little sound that evoked all the emotions of the primitive. He'd settle for that, he knew. Primitive was simple. No complications. He put aside his wonderings as she slid upward along his body. His lips tasted the smoothness of one round, copper-tinted breast. The world held more, he knew, but nothing sweeter.

LOOKING FORWARD!
**The following is the opening
section from the next novel in the exciting
Trailsman series from Signet:**

**THE TRAILSMAN #224
TEXAS TINHORNS**

> *Texas, 1860—where young men were
> taught hard lessons about the merits
> of growing up quick, learning a fast
> draw, and keeping their heads down
> when the lead starts to fly. . . .*

"Whiskey," Fargo said to the bartender. "And leave
the bottle."

The sour-faced bartender slammed the bottle of
whiskey on the bar and snatched up Fargo's silver
dollar. His last, as luck would have it. He'd just come
off a twelve-hour poker game upstairs in Slim Whitmore's saloon and had dropped everything he had, almost five hundred dollars.

Fargo had been kicking around San Angelo for a few weeks, having finally gunned down a particular nasty little killer named Billy Batts, a Louisiana lowlife who'd slaughtered several families in Texas and New Mexico Territory. Batts was a scurvy scum who'd just as soon slit a child's throat as squash a mosquito on his arm. The reward for his capture—preferably dead rather than alive—had swelled to a thousand dollars after Batts had slaughtered a rancher and his family near El Paso. Then Fargo caught up with him.

The thousand dollars was gone. Fargo had already squandered it on whiskey and women and clean sheets and some solid meals and gambling.

Fargo sipped his whiskey and watched the two young guys down at the end of the bar, tinhorns both and no mistake. They were laughing too loud, paying for everyone's drinks for no reason, and enjoying themselves far too much. In west Texas, fun was always in short supply. Men drank for anything but.

"Another round on the house, innkeeper," the taller of the two called out.

While there were a couple of takers to the boys' offer of a round, they were looked at with distrust by the majority of customers: grizzled, sun-baked west Texans who were suspicious of their own noses. They didn't cotton to strangers, especially ones with flat-toned Eastern accents, boots that were too shiny new, and britches with no dirt on them.

"Drink up, boys," the shorter of the pair squealed as the bartender poured brown rotgut into shot glasses up and down the bar. The shorter tinhorn was slapping the drinkers on the back cheerfully. None responded with more than an annoyed nod or grunt.

The bartender tilted the bottle to pour a shot into an empty glass. Before the shotglass stood a tall, stocky, unshaven man with teeth brown from chewing tobacco and about a month's worth of trail dust covering him from head to toe.

The man put a callused, beefy hand over the shot glass, and the bartender poured booze all over the man's knuckles.

Fargo watched, knowing what was coming.

When a man was looking hard enough for a fight, odds were good he'd find one.

"I can pay fer my own whiskey," the big man growled, not looking up but making sure the two tinhorns could hear him.

He shook the whiskey from his hand and said, louder this time, "And I sure as shit don't take no drinks from any Eastern peckerwoods."

The challenge, undoubtedly, was now officially thrown down.

The two tinhorns, Fargo saw, seemed uncertain how to respond. The shorter one walked back to his friend. They started talking softly to each other. Fargo could hear most of it.

"I think we've just been insulted," the shorter one said. "I didn't understand all his words, but the ones I did weren't very nice.

"No, they weren't," the taller one said. "Do you have any ideas on how we should handle this?" the shorter one asked. "Remember that book we read, *Shoot-out at Snake Gulch*?" the tall one said. "remember what Hardcase McCoy did in the Fancy Lady Saloon?"

"Didn't he—" the short one started.

"—kill the desperado," the tall one finished. He was smiling, looking kind of dreamy as he remembered. "It was in a place just like this, Corny. Hardcase McCoy draws his Colt and pumps three shots into the guy's head."

"That was a book, Ferdie," the shorter one said. "This is real."

The taller tinhorn, Ferdie, having decided he'd just been slighted, was glaring at the stocky stranger now.

He said, "Hardcase McCoy wasn't afraid of anyone, and neither am I."

"Ferdie, I don't think—"

Ferdie ignored Corny and walked out into the middle of the floor. Fargo sighed tiredly and put his drink back on the bar. This kid was even dumber than he looked.

New spurs clanging, the Easterner brushed the tips of his fingers over the butts of his pistols—which had yet to be fired, Fargo knew instinctively—and said, "Don't believe I like your subtext of hostility, stranger."

Fargo groaned. Either this kid had a death wish or he actually believed he could out-draw the stocky man. The kid would go belly up with a half-pound of lead in his gut.

The big man grabbed his empty shot glass and flung it away, where it narrowly missed some poker players at a table. He turned toward Ferdie, ready and eager to ventilate the skinny young bastard.

He kicked a bar stool over and took some steps toward Ferdie. The place got quiet enough to hear a rattlesnake fart.

The shorter guy was quaking in his boots, watching his friend walking into certain death.

"I don't like you or your fancy-ass words," the stranger said, murder in his gray eyes. "You come into my town with your snake-oil Yankee ways, and your blood money made off the sweat and toil of good God-fearin' Texans. An' you think you can make it better by buyin' me a lousy drink?" He eyed Ferdie with murderous rage. "Anytime yer ready to settle the score, you go fer it.'

The smaller guy suddenly got his dander up and darted over to the stranger. He said, "The seriousness of your claims is not in dispute here, sir—"

The stranger shoved Corny aside, and Corny went flying into the piano player, sending them both crashing to the sawdust-covered floor.

"Draw, you Yankee bastard," the stranger said, and went for his gun.

Fargo took over. Before the tall tinhorn could even clear leather, Fargo was firing at the stranger. Two shots rang out and the stranger, in mid draw, looked startled as two holes opened in his chest. Before he could react further, he dropped his pistol and fell back against the bar. He slumped to the floor, his eyes staying open in surprise even as death washed over him.

Fargo twirled his Colt into his holster. Ferdie was still clutching the butt of his gun, never having even drawn his weapon, staring at the dead man in shock.

"D-did I do that?" he asked no one in particular.

"No," Corny said, still laying on the floor. "It was him."

He pointed to Fargo, who was turning back to the bar. Ferdie gawked at Fargo, who was pouring himself a shot.

He glanced down at the big stranger's lifeless body, which was already drawing flies. Ferdie had never actually seen a real dead person. And this guy was definitely dead. Only when saliva began dribbling down his chin did Ferdie realize that his mouth was hanging open in amazement.

Corny, still flat on his butt, likewise stared at the lifeless form sprawled on the dusty bar room floor.

"Do I know you, stranger?" Ferdie asked.

"Name's Fargo, Skye Fargo," he said, "but you can call me Hardcase McCoy if you're of a mind to."

"I didn't need your help, Mr. Fargo," Ferdie said.

"Yes, you did," Fargo replied, turning away from the boys to concentrate on his drink.

Corny scrambled to his feet, leaving the piano player flat on his back. Corny rushed over to his friend. "Are you all right, Ferdie?" he asked.

Ferdie ignored him. He said to Fargo, "I could have taken him."

"The hell you say," Fargo said, sipping his whiskey. "Gunslingin' don't afford you no second chance. Your dead friend over there had you hands down."

"You say—" Ferdie snapped. "I'm greased lightening with a gun."

"You couldn't grease your own pecker with a pound of Limburger cheese," Fargo said.

Fargo saw a look of anger cross the young Yankee's

face. He opened his mouth to speak, but his friend grabbed him and said to Fargo, "Don't pay him any of your mind, sir. We appreciate what you did."

Ferdie jerked his arm free. He said to Fargo, "I didn't need you fighting my battles."

"Ferdie," the shorter one said. "He saved your bacon. That man would've killed you."

"I was doing fine till he came along," Ferdie said angrily, kicking at the sawdust like a pissy little boy. Fargo sipped his whiskey nonchalantly.

"Can we buy you a drink, mister?" the shorter guy asked. "A bottle if you want it."

"A bottle?" Ferdie asked indignantly. "You want to buy this man a bottle? After he stole my kill? Are you crazy, Corny?"

Fargo finished the last of his whiskey and turned to the two young men.

"No thanks," he said to Corny. "I've had enough for now. But I don't think you have."

He hitched up his pants and wiped his mouth with his sleeve. He sauntered over to the swinging bar doors, and said to them, "You best come with me now, boys. We got some things to discuss."

"What things?" Ferdie wanted to know.

"Like how to stay alive," Fargo said. "I'll be over at the cafe whenever you're ready."

He disappeared out the door. Ferdie turned to the bartender and said, "Who is that man?"

"You heard," the bartender said. "Skye Fargo. And if you boys have half a brain between ya, y'all will get your asses over to the cafe."

Corny looked at his friend and said, "I do believe he's right, Ferdie."

Ferdie said, "Whose side are you on, anyway?"

"Yours," Corny said, grabbing his friend's arm and dragging him out of the saloon.

"You two ain't from around here, are you?" Fargo said to them, wiping up the last of the beef-stew gravy with a crust of bread.

"No, we're not," Corny said. "How'd you know?"

"My guess would be New York, maybe Baltimore, maybe Philadelphia," Fargo said. "But if I had to, I'd put my money on New York."

"You're very observant, Mr. Fargo," Ferdie said. "New York is correct."

"I thought so," Fargo said.

"What gave us away?" Corny wanted to know.

"The way you walk, the way you talk, the way you don't seem to know your asses from your toenails."

An aging, white-haired woman came doddering over to the table carrying a tray. On it was one solitary cup of coffee, which she plopped down in front of Fargo, sloshing some onto his lap. She tossed the battered tray onto a table and said to Ferdie and Corny, "You boys want somethin' to eat or are you here to feast on my beauty?"

"What kind of seafood does this establishment offer?" Corny asked her. "Can I get some sautéed blue snapper?"

"I can give you fried catfish, fried beefsteak, and chili and stew," the old gal said.

"Bring 'em two blueplate specials, Miranda," Fargo

said to her, wiping coffee from his lap with a napkin. "And put them on my tab."

"If you say so," Miranda said wearily, and shuffled back to the kitchen.

"What exactly is a blueplate special?" Ferdie asked.

"After you eat it, you turn blue," Fargo said.

"Why did you help us, Mr. Fargo?" the short guy, Corny, asked. "We didn't ask for your help."

"You didn't have to," Fargo said. "But you needed it all the same." He sipped his coffee. "Do I speak the truth?"

"I think maybe you do," Corny said. "We're new to these parts."

Fargo said, "The question is, why are you here?"

"Why shouldn't we be here?" Ferdie asked somewhat testily.

"Cause you both stick out like a skunk in whorehouse," Fargo said to them. "Let me guess: you both are a couple of Eastern dudes who've read too many books and believe the slop those Yankee hacks pour onto the page. Let me set you fellers straight: what those writers say rarely ever happens, and when it does, they're never around to see."

Ferdie and Corny looked at each other, uncertain.

"Supposing you're correct, Fargo," Ferdie said. "Then what?"

Miranda toddled out of the steamy kitchen carrying a tray with two plates on it. She set them down on the table before the Yankees. The aroma of burnt pork chops wafted up at them.

"Then nothing," Fargo said. "If you boys got an ounce of smarts, you'll hightail it back to the bosom of your families. A smart sheep never strays far from the flock."

"We have money," Ferdie said, taking a stab at the pork chop. The fork bounced off. "Lots of it."

"Never knew a bankroll that could stop a bullet," Fargo said.

"What I meant was," Ferdie said, "you look like someone who can teach us everything we need to know about being real men of the West."

Corny nodded in agreement and said, "That's right, Mr. Fargo. You could teach us how to shoot, and ride a horse, and lasso a steer and chew tobacco, just like Charlie Siringo, the stove-up Texas cowboy. We read about him in a book."

Fargo smiled at them as one would a couple of mischievous children. "What those New York pulp writers don't tell is what it's really like bein' a cowboy. Charlie Siringo wasn't just stove up, his kidneys were shuttin' down on him from a steady diet of beans and bourbon. He looked sixty when he was thirty, his feet were so bad from wearin' boots even his corns had corns, and he had piles from sitting atop a horse all day long." Fargo sipped his coffee. He said, "That what you boys want?"

"What we want," Ferdie said, "is a taste of the cowboy life, not a career."

"And it should be a fun taste," Corny put in.

"We'll give you five hundred dollars," Ferdie said, "and money for expenses, whatever comes up."

Fargo couldn't help but look interested. He said, "You got that kind of money on you?"

Ferdie pulled a billfold from his pants pocket and

counted out five hundred, dropping the bills on the table.

"Do we have a deal?" Ferdie asked.

Fargo said, "If you can pay me five hundred, you can probably afford seven-fifty."

Ferdie looked at his friend quizzically. Corny leaned over and whispered something in Ferdie's ear. Ferdie whispered something back. Corny shook his head. Ferdie looked exasperated, then counted out five fifties from the billfold.

"Seven-fifty," Ferdie said, a little snidely. "Care to count it?"

"I'll count it when there's a thousand on the table," Fargo said.

"A thousand?" Ferdie gasped.

"I would've settled for seven-fifty," Fargo said to Ferdie, "but then I decided that with such a bad attitude, as you have it's gonna cost you an extra two-fifty."

"That's a little high," Ferdie said.

"Heaven is higher," Fargo said, "and there's a good chance you'll be spendin' some time there with that right smart mouth of yours." Fargo rose from his chair and jammed his hat on his head. "My price is one thousand dollars. That's five hundred dollars per ass, both of which I think I'll be a-savin' from certain death."

He tossed fifty cents onto the table for his meal. His last fifty cents. There was seven hundred and fifty dollars there for the taking but, Fargo knew, money talked louder when a man was prepared to walk away from it.

Fargo went toward the door. He could hear the Easterners arguing in hushed tones. Corny said, "It's worth the extra money. He *did* save our lives, after all."

They argued back and forth for a moment.

"Tether your horse, Mr. Fargo," Ferdie finally said, plopping more bills on the pile. "One thousand dollars. And we'd better have lots and lots of fun."

Fargo scooped up the money. Barring any unforeseen circumstances—like women and poker—Fargo could live on a thousand dollars for a high-on-the-hog month or two. Maybe even six months, if he lived clean.

"Just bought yourself a teacher, boys," Fargo said. He jammed the money into his pocket and sat down again.

"So," he said, "what would you guys like to do first?"

Ferdie leaned over and whispered again in Corny's ear. Corny nodded. Ferdie turned to Fargo and said, "We'd really like to rob a bank."